POWER OF THE PIE

BY: MARENDA

Power of the Pie

-A Novel Written by-

Marenda Powell

Cover Design: Dynasty CoverMe

Editor: Joy Nelson

Acknowledgments

I first have to give thanks to my heavenly father for blessing me with the gift to write. My lovely husband, family and friends. This book is dedicated to my friends, family, and supporters. You all have supported me in many ways from providing me with the space to write, pushing me to complete my book, and taking the time to read my novel and giving me your input. Because of you all, I am fulfilling my life's dream to be a writer.

Prologue

Alicia went into the motel to pay for the room, the lady at the front desk handed her the key to the room Lamont had reserved. Leaving the girls in the room they got with the men. Christina acted as if she was going to the vending machine for some ice, looking back to make sure she wasn't being followed.

On the way back from the ice machine, she stopped at the room Jack and the crew were hanging out in. Knowing she couldn't be gone for too long without anyone noticing. Christina went to the room where Jack and the fellas were getting ready, took off her shirt and put on some body armor. Then she tucked one .38 under her skirt and another one in her purse.

When Christina made it back to the girls, the music was blasting and Sariya was at the sink mixing up the drinks. Walking over, Christina handed Sariya the ice, then turned around to look at Alicia.

"I think I had too much to drink." Alicia rose to her feet and rushed off to the bathroom.

Christina went in after her making sure to grab her purse, saying as loud as she could, "Sis, you alright?" Then she closed the door behind her.

Snap knocked on the door "You okay, baby girl?"

"I'm cool, just too much Patron. I'll be out in a minute," Alicia assured him.

Going into her purse, Christina handed Alicia a strap, then walked back into the room. Each person had a glass in their hand and Sariya walked around making sure the men's drinks stayed filled to the rim.

Marcus started to become impatient, he was ready to jump deep into Sariya's pussy. Pulling her to him forcefully, he tongue kissed her. The kiss made her think of all the times at Treasure Island that she had been raped. Thinking about her past, she bit down on his tongue.

Marcus jumped up and yelled, "Bitch, what the fuck you bite me for?"

Sariya smiled, "I thought you liked it rough, daddy."

Marcus charged towards her, ready to smack the smile off her face, but he was pulled back by Snap and Kris. Snap knew Marcus had a bad temper and word around the hood was that he had a habit of beating up women.

Snap pulling Marcus back calmed him down and not wanting to go to jail for fucking this bitch up. Marcus excused his self and went

2

to get some air. For a second, Sariya started to panic. She went to follow him to apologize, but as she walked outside she saw Cliff already talking to him and smoking on a cigarette. Cliff looked her way and gave her a nod to go back to the room.

Chapter 1

For years, women and children had been captured by a group of men. On a hot summer day a group of young girls were on 90th and Mac Arthur, getting some things for their 4th of July barbeque. Suddenly, some men jumped out of a van and grabbed three teenagers along with Jordan's kid sisters.

They took them to an exclusive location off of Treasure Island, which had been shut down by the authorities for a long time. For years the girls had been held hostage, forced to live there against their will. They had been used as prostitutes, made to sleep with random men in the city. They had thought about escaping, but were too afraid of Trent also known as Danger. Trent was well known in the street as a Drug Lord, but also a very dangerous man. Rumors were that he was mentally not all there in the head. By looking at him you would think he was the perfect gentlemen. He stood 6'1 with a smooth chocolate complexion, body built like a brick house and he always was dressed to impress. Trent was abandoned at a young age and felt his mother betrayed him. She chose a man over him and every since then Trent had it in his head that woman were nothing but hoes and tricks.

The Women had known for years that these men had been kidnaping woman and young girls and getting away with it. If the women they'd kidnapped became old and no one wanted to sleep with them any longer, the kidnappers would kill them and keep if any of the woman had children. They would stay at Treasure Island until they were ready to put in some work.

At night the women would silently plot their escape. Because of the prostitution they were forced into, they had learned a lot about how to trick men and make them crumble at their feet by using their body.

Trent had a thing for Jordan due to the fact she was thick as shit, ass like Serena Williams with a mocha complexion and light green eyes. Jordan was one of the many woman who was kidnapped in Oakland and hell against her will. She come from a big family, a father who adored her and a mother that would go above and beyond for her. So many nights Trent would take her for himself, he rarely allowed anyone to pay for Jordan because he wanted her. Trent figure that one day he might want children, with him and Jordan looks, it would make a good combination for a kid.

One night Snow snuck into the office and did some research on how to kill, she learned a lot. Snow got it the worst due to the fact she was white, and the men took their anger of being tortured by the police and white men out on her. What they didn't know was that their

5

abuse just made her stronger. She vowed that if she ever escaped she was paying all those muthafuckas that kidnapped and raped her back.

Jordan had a date with the main man for the night, Alexis was still on a date with a client. Jordan had talked Trent into taking a candle light bath. She suggested, "Let me cater to you, boo."

While he was in the bath, Jordan prepared dinner. She had learned how to make arsenic and had cooked it in the meatloaf. She had been feeding it to him for weeks in his food and it was causing stomach problems that would inevitably leave him to die silently and in pain. It would eat his body up from the inside out. And to top things off, she added anti-freeze to his margarita.

"Trent, come on, baby, before the dinner gets hot"

Trent shouted, "Bitch, don't rush me. And I am not your baby, I'm your boss."

"Okay, I was just saying that dinner is ready. I know how you don't like cold food."

Trent had gotten out of the bath and began to dig into his food. He finally looked up.

"Sit down and eat!" He barked and Jordan sat down and began to eat. She made sure not to put the poison in her food and sat there eating like she didn't have a care in the world.

For the first time in a long time she had a reason to smile. She was going to pay back every muthafucka that had something to do with kidnapping her, her friends, and the children.

She sat quietly and watched the poison start to kick in, watched the sweat begin to drip down Trent's face. Jordan couldn't help it any longer and suddenly a smile was plastered on her face.

"Bitch, why you sitting over there so happy for?"

Jordan replied while smiling, "No reason, I'm just enjoying this last meal with you."

"Last meal? You will eat with me as much as I say. The fuck you thought? You belong to me until I'm tired of you. Act right and you don't have to worry about that. I might make you my baby momma," Trent laughed.

Jordan burst out laughing. "Your baby momma? I can't believe it! You want me to be your baby momma? I am so honored."

"Shut the fuck up with all the drama and let me finish eating, matter of fact, make me some more," said Trent.

She got up from the table, loaded his plate with another serving of food, and topped off his margarita. The anticipation of watching him die was killing her.

"Trent, I thought you wanted some of this pie?" Jordan questioned.

She then went over to the couch, opened her legs, sprayed some whipped cream there, and gave him a full view. After having eaten all of the food that had been prepared, Trent staggered over to her. He bent down and started eating her pie like it was his last meal. In all reality, it was. After two orgasms, Jordan laid Trent down and began to ride his dick.

"Trent, look at me while I ride this big ass dick. You like this pussy?" Jordan asked.

"Hell yeah! This shit is hella wet, got a nigga sweating and shit."

"You're not sweating over being in this pussy. You want to know why you're sweating?"

"Damn, bitch, since when talking while having sex is fun? Shut the fuck up!"

"But you want to hear this. Look at me, Trent, you're sweating because you are dying."

"J, you had too much to drink. Go on with that shit and let me bust this nut," Trent demanded.

"Trent, listen to me. You're dying. You thought you were going to get away with kidnapping girls and that nothing would ever happen to you. You're quiet, you feel it now? It's called Arsenic, it's eating up your insides," Jordan smiled.

Trent pushed her off of him and tried to lunge at her, but he was too weak. All he could do was lay there with his dick out.

"I told you," Jordan bragged.

"Fuck you! Bitch, you won't get away with it!" Trent yelled.

Jordan replied "Oh, but I will. Now shut the fuck up you pathetic muthafucka. Die already so I can go get my girls and get the fuck out of here."

Within minutes, he took his last breath. He was finally gone. Jordan knew where he kept his stash of money and his straps. She quickly got dressed and strapped up on her way to save the other women.

Looking around the room before she crept out, she noticed the bag with the keys of coke hadn't been picked up yet. Deciding to take that too, she slung it over her shoulder and was on the move.

A few exits away from Treasure Island, Snow was caked up with a detective. He was one of her regulars and tonight he was trying to convince her to go away with him. She had considered it until she thought of her sisters back at that hellhole.

Snow was a beautiful woman. She stood five feet six inches with light blue eyes and long sandy brown hair. She had wide hips and huge breasts which drove the men crazy.

Detective Leon would give her extra money on the side, minus paying for her services, just in case she ever decided to escape. In a way, Snow had taken a liking to Leon, but she had no place for love in her heart. That had been taken away from her the moment she was kidnapped. Tonight was the night the girls had planned to escape. If timing was right, Trent was already taken care of.

While Leon was in the bathroom, Snow jammed the door from the outside so that Leon couldn't escape and then spent off with his wallet and keys. Exiting Treasure Island and pulling to the side, Snow hopped out and changed her clothes. Then she checked her piece to make sure it was loaded.

Going into Leon's trunk, she spotted a twelve gauge and a bullet proof vest. Leaving Leon's car on the road and hoping over the fence, Snow crawled to the main house where she and Jordan were supposed to meet up.

"Sis, Sis!" Snow whispered.

"Crawl to the side." Jordan responded.

"You already taken care of Trent?" Snow asked, looking through the window where Alexis was.

"Hell yeah, that bitch ass nigga is down."

"You ready?" Snow questioned.

Jordan didn't even reply, she was already ducking and diving behind trees on her way to rescue her sister.

There were two men standing guard, one in the front and one in the back. They always stayed close by when some of the girls were with certain tricks. Snow thought she was a professional hit man and she took out a small, sharp machete and threw it at the men standing out front. It hit one of them on the side of his neck.

Once the girls saw that, they both hurried to where he was, and pulled him to the side of the building. The guard was still grasping for air as Jordan took the machete out of his neck. Pulling out the .45 with the silencer on it, she let off two shots. One to the head and one to the chest. After they assured he was dead, they rolled him down the hill that went off into the water.

Continuing with their mission, slowly they crept to the back of the house and realized that the gunman wasn't even paying attention to his surroundings. Snow was thankful for the silencer on the gun she had taken from the other guard. When she looked around to make sure no one would notice, she pointed the weapon at the man's head and fired, but missed, hitting him in the shoulder.

He was on full alert at that point and tried to call for help. Before he could, Alexis came out of the back door aiming a .45 at his head and shot him point blank.

POW! POW!

"That's my bitch!" Snow juiced.

"Come on, we still have to get Raine and Sariya," Alexis said.

"Were not going to help any of the other women?" Snow asked.

"Whoever is in the room with the kids, we will try to take them too. But, sis, we have to go before the other dudes come back?" Jordan admitted.

Raine and Sariya were waiting patiently for their sisters to come and rescue them. As instructed, they were able to poison the men, but it hadn't yet killed them.

"Hurry up and put on your shoes and jacket, they'll be here any second," Raine muttered.

"But, Raine, the poison hasn't kicked in," Sariya whimpered.

"Don't worry about that, just get ready," said Raine.

Waiting nervously in their room for the signal, they suddenly heard a thump. Gazing out of the window, they saw one of the men out front, bent over.

"Sariya, Raine?" Jordan whispered.

"Were in here," they replied.

Jordan walked into the room and snatched them both up. There were only three other girls in the center with them.

"Okay, once we all walk out of this door, I need everyone to stay low and in the middle of us. Once we make it to the gate, hop over, there is a car waiting for us," Alexis said, checking her strap.

They had thirty minutes to make it out of the camp before the men came back. Ducking and dodging, trying to avoid the other men who were left to watch the grounds, they were mere feet away from the gate. Snow hopped over first as Alexis helped the younger girls go over one by one.

Once over the gate, they all rushed to the car. The car was only so big, so they had to sit one on top of the other so that they would all fit inside. Driving down the long road, they noticed a car headed towards the camp. Not wanting the occupants of the other car to look their way, the girls drove, trying not to look suspicious.

Finally making it to the freeway and across the bridge, they headed towards Sacramento, the opposite direction from where their family was and from where the men that had kidnapped them were from.

Chapter 2

"So what's the plan now?" Snow asked.

"We have to get out of dodge and get rid of this car," Jordan said.

An hour and a half later, taking an exit in Sacramento to an unfamiliar area, they found a motel. Snow used her looks and flirted with the clerk, talking him in letting them check in without identification. Jordan, Alexis and Snow checked everyone in and left instructions for them to not call anyone or answer the door. Then they left.

The girls drove down highway 80, taking the car Snow had stolen from the detective to Discovery Park and setting the vehicle on fire. Afterwards, they walked up Garden Highway, back to the motel.

When they arrived, the girls were still sitting on the beds with their clothes on, extremely shaken up.

"I know everyone is hungry, Snow grab the yellow pages and order us some pizzas and something to drink. No need to be scared, ladies. We are free from them bastards and I'm for damn sure gon' make them all regret the day they took us. Smile," Jordan preached.

"So what's next?" Raine asked.

"First thing in the morning we're going shopping to get a change of clothes. Then we'll bring you girls back here while we go find somewhere permanent to live. Sacramento will be our new hometown, it's the best place for us to lay low and make it," Alexis suggested.

Suddenly there was a knock at the door. It was just the pizza man, but it had them on edge, they were all still jumpy from escaping.

The next morning each lady woke, put their clothes from the night before back on and headed to Walmart for some under clothes and Ross' to get a few things.

Snow, Jordan, and Alexis got the girls back to the motel and settled, then headed out to meet up with some people. They were trying to get rid of the keys of coke and to get some identification.

Alexis had a friend back in the Bay she could reach out to and she wouldn't have to worry about it getting back to Greg or his crew. This friend was the one man she could trust, more like a big brother. In the hood they called him Mick, but she knew him as Makai.

Stopping at the gas station payphone across the street from the motel, Alexis called his number. The first time he didn't answer, on the second time around he finally picked up.

"Makai, this me, Lexi. I really need your help, but it has to stay between me and you," Alexis whispered.

"Lexi? Girl, where the fuck you been?" Makai hollered.

14

"Can't get into all that. Can you meet me in Sac?" She asked.

"Give me a few hours, I'll swoop down there," Makai confirmed.

Walking back to the motel and waiting for Makai to arrive, all the girls were nervous, unsure if Alexis' brother could be trusted.

"Sis, you sure he's coming?" Snow asked. Immediately following her question, there was a knock on the door.

"Who is it?" Jordan yelled.

"It's me, open the door," Makai said as he walked in, leaving one of his men at the door.

Alexis rushed to give him a hug as the tears began to flow. It had been a long time since she'd seen a familiar, loving face.

"Sis, what's going on? And where have you been?" Makai questioned.

"I... Well, we were all kidnapped and held captive over the past few years. Thank God you have the same number. I wasn't sure who I could trust. We escaped. You can't tell nobody I'm alive, not yet at least."

"So what you need me to do?" Makai asked.

"When we escaped, I took these keys," she gestured to the bag that held the drugs. "How much can we get for them? I also need some hook up so we can get somewhere to live, like stubs and identification." Alexis rambled.

Makai walked over to the bag and broke off a piece of the key. Rubbing some of the residue from the coke on his gums, instantly they went numb.

"How many keys you got?" Makai asked, eager.

"A bag full," Alexis admitted, gesturing for Jordan to bring it over.

"I have my own connect, but I'll buy these off you. How much you want for them?" Makai asked.

"Bruh, I have never sold drugs before. What can you give me?" Alexis asked.

"Usually I wouldn't pay more than seventeen stacks a key, but since you're sis and this shit on point, I'll shoot you eighteen-five. I don't have that much on me right now, though. Tomorrow I'll shoot back out here with the dough and the other info you need."

Makai took the bag and headed to the door, then he threw her his phone, letting her know he would hit her when he was on his way.

The next day it was hot as hell in Sac. The girls all went for a swim, patiently waiting for Makai to come back with their dough and their info. Snow went to use the computer at the Kinko's close by the motel and came across a couple of homes that were nice and in quiet areas where they wouldn't have to worry about being noticed.

Alexis hoped she was right about her big brother because they only had enough cash to get them by for a little bit longer. Ten keys at eighteen-five a key would put them in a good position to be able to survive and put their plan in full motion.

After spending all day stressing, five o'clock arrived and there was still no word from Makai. By that time, each of the girls had fallen asleep, full of worry.

"Sis, Sis, the phone going off." Snow shook Alexis to wake her up.

"Hello?"

"Come to the door," Makai demanded.

Makai didn't stay for long, though. He stayed only long enough to give Alexis a bag full of money, two hundred thousand to be exact. She was filled with excitement and had never seen so much money in her life. He also gave her contact information to a dude that did all of the illegal paperwork she needed, plus he would hook her up with a ride.

"Oh, my God! I can't believe we have all this money," Alexis hollered.

"If it wasn't for you, J, we would be ass out. You did your thing," Snow chimed.

"I almost left them. We should be straight for a while," Jordan was ecstatic.

That night, after the younger girls were asleep, Alexis, Jordan and Snow went to meet the connect Mark told them about while Christina, Monica and Alicia did some research on Sac. Two buses and a light rail later they finally made it.

The car lot was on a busy street near Arden Mall. Right across the street from the bus stop stood the used car lot.

Walking into the facility, Jordan went up to the first person she saw. "Excuse me, were here to meet with Wayne?"

"Are you Alexis?"

"No, I am. These are my sisters," Alexis interrupted.

"Wayne will be back shortly. He's expecting you and informed me that you should take a look around the lot and pick out whatever you like."

It was pitch black in the place so you couldn't really make out all the cars, but they looked around anyway. Picking out something that could fit them, each agreed on the black on black 2012 Escalade. While taking it for a test drive, Alexis almost crashed, but she soon got the hang of it. By the time they made it back to the lot, Wayne had arrived.

"So how much?" Snow asked.

"It's on sale for fifteen, but I can give it to you for thirteen cash," Wayne answered.

"What about the other information?" Jordan asked.

"Shelly, go to my office and get the paperwork. You'll find everything you need inside," Wayne advised, handing Jordan the envelope.

"Would you happen to have the hook up on some protection?" Jordan asked.

"What a pretty little thing like you need a gun for?" Wayne questioned.

"Is that a yes or no?" Snow asked, agitated.

"Come to the back," Wayne ushered them.

Wayne's used cars proved to be a one stop shop for the women.

Waking up the following the day and gathering their belongings, Alexis drove around to find them a place to call their own. At the first few places, the owners weren't going for it, they weren't interested in selling.

Then they came across the perfect six bedroom house. By luck the owner was a single old man and the amount he was being offered upfront was something he couldn't refuse. Signing the paper work, the girls were all excited. They had just gone from hostages to homeowners.

Immediately following the purchase of their home, their next stop was to a furniture store where they chose their bedroom sets and the women decorated the living room and dining room together as a family.

Finally settled into their new home in Sacramento, Jordan thought it was time for the older women to go out and celebrate. Going to Arden Mall with the crew, they all went their own way to find something to wear for the night.

Meeting up at the food court, some young guy came up to Snow, giving her a flyer to an event in downtown Sac. After leaving the mall, the next stop was the salon, all the girls were getting hooked up. Some girls in the food court at the mall were talking about a shop off of Watt, so the women decided to head there.

Driving down the street towards the shop, the blade was packed with young woman trying to make there coins.

"This where we need to be. They're hoeing anyway, so why not make some real dough and have somewhere to live too? Let's come back this way on our way to the house," Jordan said.

"Good idea. Plus, that's how we can make our money, recruit some of the hottest chicks and set them up on dates. Get this money the best way we know how," Alexis chimed in.

Hours later, the ladies were whipped and dipped. Snow got blonde highlights and long layers. Jordan got a layer cut, black with burgundy highlights to bring out her mocha color. Alexis rocked a short haircut, jet black. Alicia had long dreads down to her ass, she got her locks touched up and the tips died burnt orange.

Christina was Puerto Rican with hair that cascaded down her back. She decided on changing her color to a light shade of brown with highlights and low lights. Monica let the hair stylist talk her into going blonde, said it would go good with her light skin and light brown eyes. Along with the color she went with a short cut styled into a Mohawk and the front long and pulled away from her face. Sariya and Raine settled on a wrap with their natural colors.

After they were done at the salon, the ladies rode up on some Asian chick standing on the corner with her shoes leaning. Alexis got out of the car an approached the girl who looked to be no more than twenty-two. She was cute, though. Five feet three inches, long red hair, and from the looks of it she wasn't making any money.

Lexi walked up to her. "Hey, I'm Lexi. And you are?"

Red looked Alexis up and down. "Um... They call me Red. I'm working, but um...what can I do for you?"

"It's not what you can do for me, it's what I can do for you. There's no way your happy with how your boss got you walking out here with your shoes leaning. You're way too pretty to be on the blade. Come get down with me and my ladies, you'll make major loot and never walk the blade again. What do you say?" Alexis inquired.

"Shit, you don't have to tell me twice," Red hollered.

"Let's roll." Before heading back to the house, Jordan pulled up to Macy's to get Red something to wear for the night.

Back at home, all of the women followed their usual tradition, each cooking a dish and having dinner together. Seafood was the meal of choice with peach cobbler for desert. Afterwards, Snow showed Red to her room and headed off to go get ready for the evening.

Meeting in the family room, each girl was dressed to impress. Jordan wore black tuxedo shorts to accentuate her ass. She also wore a blazer, a black Victoria's Secret bombshell bra and black Red Bottoms. Alexis wore a short black Bebe dress with a slit down the front. She allowed her breasts to hang freely, covering only her nipple. And she topped her ensemble off with black and pink Jimmy Choo's.

Snow decided on a white lace cat suit with a hint of light pink. She added light pink Prada's heals and a dash of make-up. Monica and the other girls decided on staying in for the night.

"Okay, ladies, let's have a good time. Let's make sure we stay in each other's eyesight. And, Red, you will stay with me. I'll say this one time, if you cross us you'll regret it. I gave you my word that I will ensure you work, get some dough, and have a place to stay," Alexis warned.

Old Sac was moving, clubs on every corner. The girls parked in a garage and walked up. Many had come out to support the performers, there were people standing around the block trying to get in. Snow got to the front of the line and whispered something in the security guards ear. Whatever she said got them in the club and with a bottle service added.

Next to them were some dudes with tricks giving them lap dances. Turning up, not caring who was paying them any mind, one of the rappers walked up to Jordan, asking if he could get a dance. Her first reaction was hell no, then she took another glance at him and realized he was breathtaking.

His name was Isaac and he stood six feet, two inches tall with light brown eyes. Judging by the way his clothes fit, he was very athletic with the smoothest chocolate skin. Isaac laughed at the gorgeous woman that was about to object until she took notice of him. Watching her reaction, he could tell that she was intrigued, but not on that groupie shit.

"I never seen you out here before. Where you from?" Isaac asked.

"Let's just say not I'm from here, new to town," Jordan replied.

"Can I see you after this?" Isaac asked.

"Do I come off like that type of girl? I'm going home."

"I'm talking about hitting up IHOP or something. I don't want our night to end."

"Let me see if my girls wants to roll," Jordan told him as she walked off.

Everyone agreed on going out to eat with Isaac and his friends. Alexis thought it would be good for business, she'd found out that the men were in the music industry, well known artists who were getting their coins.

IHOP was packed like it was the after hour spot.

"What brings you ladies to Sac?" Isaac asked.

Before she could reply, a group of woman took notice of Isaac, a.k.a 4-5, his rap name. The women asked for an autograph. He looked over towards Jordan and she gave him a nod, letting him know she didn't mind.

"A change of scenery, plus it's mad cheap to live here and a good place for our kind of business," Alexis replied.

"What kind of business?" Jimmy asked.

"We have an escort service. So if you ever need some high-end, sexy women, or if you know of anyone, hit my line," Jordan said.

When Alexis informed them of what kind of business they were in, the men looked shocked, but impressed. Isaac said he needed a few women for his video shoot the following week and Jordan advised him on taking a look at the women so he could chose his preference. They hadn't been in Sac a month yet and they were already making connections.

Snow excused herself to the restroom, she'd seen a familiar face. She crept to the truck to cop her pistol then she stood outside of the men's restroom and out walked one of the men who worked at the Treasure Island camp.

"Hey, remember me?" Snow whispered with a devious smile.

"What the fuck? How you escape?" Adam asked.

"Don't worry about that. Make your way back to the bathroom and if you reach for anything, I will blow your fucking head off," Snow assured him.

Walking back into the bathroom, Snow checked all of the stalls, making sure no one was in there to witness what she was getting ready to do. Holding the gun to his head, she reached in her pocket and sent Alexis a text telling her to come into the men's bathroom.

"Bitch, what you doing in here?" Alexis whispered.

"Look over there," Snow pointed.

"Muthafucka!" Alexis yelled, ran over and socked Adam square in the face.

"For years this muthafucka tortured us! Go out to the car and bring me some rope," Snow said.

Alexis rushed off to the car and came back with rope and her machete.

Adam pleaded, "You don't have to do this, you can let me go."

Snow tied his arms behind his back and pulled down his pants. Looking up towards his face, she grinned and stroked his dick until it got hard. Then she smirked.

Snow took the tape out of her bag and taped his mouth shut. Taking the machete from Alexis with one hand, she held his dick with the other hand. Then she swung down hard, slicing his dick off.

WAM!

Adam cried out as tears cascaded down his face and blood squirted everywhere. Alexis realized they were in a public place and anyone could walk in and catch them. She put her silencer on her 45 and let out two shots, one to his head. BOOM! And one to the chest. BOOM! Wiping down the door and washing up, Adam was left there in a puddle of blood.

Back at the table, Snow acted as if she wasn't feeling well and called it a night.

Arriving back at home, Alexis finally told Jordan what happened at the restaurant. Jordan was pissed because she hadn't been there to witness the death of one of the men who'd made her life a living hell over the years.

Chapter 3

The video shoot was in Ranch Cordova. Jordan took Red, Christina and Snow to Isaac so he could get a good look at them.

"Damn, J, you didn't tell me they all was bad. I want all three in the video, how much we talking about?" Isaac asked.

"Three thousand apiece for five hours. Anything over that is extra," Alexis interjected.

"You said that like I can't afford it. Hold up a second," Isaac went into his office and came out with fifteen stacks. "We'll be shooting first thing Saturday morning."

"This is more than I am charging," Jordan barked, a bit confused.

"Yeah, I know. Let's just say I might want them to stay the night," Isaac bragged.

The meeting with Isaac had gone well and was only the beginning to building there escort service. Wayne, from the car lot, had given some information on an event that was held every year in downtown Sacramento at the Marriot. He explained to the girls the place would be filled with rich men, doctors, lawyers and artist. If things went well this would put them on the map and help build their clientele.

Jordan, unlocking the door, "Okay, ladies, this event will require us all to be on point. We go in there dressed to impress and we will land some high end clients."

"We need to hit up the mall. Wayne said this is an all white event," Snow confirmed.

"Red, you think you're ready for this kind of work?" Alexis asked.

"I can handle it. Aww shit" Red hollered, looking at the news on the television.

"This is ABC news coming to you live at IHOP off of Northgate Blvd. A man has been brutally murdered here in the men's bathroom. The police have no leads and no suspects. If you have any information that may help, please call…"

The women looked at each other and smirked. Red had no idea that they were behind the killing of Adam and it was going to stay that way Throwing on some clothes and heading to Arden Mall to pick up something to wear to the ball, no one said a word. The plan was simple, one by one each man that had something to do with kidnapping them would pay.

It was the night of the all white ball. The custom dresses were designed to fit each woman perfectly, accentuating their best assets.

Snow went with a long gown that hugged her hips and trailed behind her. The back was cut low and she wore her hair in pin curls with a few curls trailing her face.

Jordan went with an all white, lace dress that stopped just above her knees. A slit at the top revealed her cleavage and some gold accessories. Alexis wore a tight white dress that showed off her curves. She wore no make-up, just nude and silver accessories.

Red decided on white tuxedo shorts, a blazer and a sheer silk top. Only a little bit of make-up was applied to her face. Christina was the youngest in the crew and a bit shy. She went simple, wearing a white, knee length dress which had a little fluff at the bottom. She donned BCBG heels and gold accessories.

Monica and Alicia stayed at the house with Sariya and Raine. Not that they weren't old enough to be left alone, but Jordan felt it was too soon and didn't want to chance them doing anything foolish and getting them caught.

"Okay, ladies, let's have some fun. Remember to spread the word, flirt a little, and if they're with someone, they might be the best clients. Nothing like a married man whose wife can't get him off," Snow recommended and laughed.

"I'm nervous," Christina admitted.

"Remember this one thing, it's power in the pie," Jordan reassured her.

"What do you mean?" Christina and Red asked.

"You have more power than you think as long as you have some good pie in between those legs. Always show confidence and you'll be okay. Never be ashamed to use what you got to get what you want," Snow said, pointing between her legs.

"Stop looking to the ground like you're unsure. You two are beautiful, let the world see you," Jordan advised.

As they pulled up to the Marriott they saw that downtown was moving with people who were turnt up for the night. Jordan led the way to the ballroom where the event was being held.

Inside, there was a live band playing soft melodies. All eyes were on them, some smiled and others were pissed because their husbands were staring so hard.

Wayne had arranged for the ladies to have a table between two other tables filled with men of high class and deep pockets. To Jordan's surprise, Dr. Johnson asked her to dance. She was surprised because he was an older white man and from the looks of his attire he was loaded with dough.

Dr. Johnson had some moves in him. Asad and Trent had made sure the girls were well trained so that they would be prepared for any clientele. Some of that training included dance lessons and even yoga and Pilates so that the ladies would be in shape and very flexible.

Jordan let it all out on the dance floor and in no time Dr. Johnson was eating out the palm of her hands, that was until some woman came and interrupted them, asking if she could cut in. By the looks of her face you could tell she was either his wife or his date for the night.

Jordan leaned into his ear and whispered, "Call me."

Dr. Johnson blushed and put the paper with Jordan's number on it in his jacket pocket without his the woman noticing. He'd never dated a black woman or a woman with so much ass and who was so bold.

Going back to the table, Jordan smiled. Watching her girls work the room, she saw that numbers were being exchanged and wives were standing on the sidelines pissed. For the ladies, business was booming.

Hours passed by and the evening ended with Christina and Red having dates for the rest of the night. Before heading off, Alexis made sure each girl had protection and Jordan jotted down the men's license plate numbers just in case shit went bad.

Jordan enjoyed being in the presence of Isaac, he made her heart smile and her pussy wet. She figured once she got her revenge on the men who had tortured her over the years, she would take Isaac up on his offer to date.

It was the day of the video shoot and Isaac had hired professional hair stylists and make-up artists.

"Isaac, you went all out. I mean, 4-5. I'm loving how my girls are looking," Jordan flirted.

"It's Isaac to you baby, 4-5 is my street name. What you thought, I wasn't going to go all out? This is my business' my way of making it," Isaac replied.

"I hear you. Where did the name 4-5 come from? If you don't mind me asking."

"I was a little shorty when I was a youngster, the name fit my height. That is until I got grown. You want to go grab something eat later?" Isaac asked.

"I told you I'm not in a place to date," Jordan responded.

"Who said it's a date? It's just two friends that's hungry. No harm in that."

Jordan finally agreed to go and eat with him at Tokyo Steak house which was close to where she lived. Everything about Isaac had Jordan wide open, his conversation, his swag, his confidence. For some he would come off to cocky, but to Jordan, a man that knew he was the shit turned her on.

"See, isn't this nice?" Isaac questioned at the steak house.

"It's cool, the food is too good."

"Admit it, you're having a good time," Isaac said.

"That, I am. This was much needed. And before I forget thank you for this lovely evening, thank you."

Isaac got serious and wanted to know more about the gorgeous woman. "Tell me about yourself."

"Not much to tell. I am from the Bay, been MIA for a few years, now I'm running an escort service and thinking of my next business venture."

"What do you like to do for fun?" Isaac asked.

"I've been gone for so long I'm not sure, but I'm open to try anything as long as it don't put my life at risk," Jordan explained.

"Let's go bowling, I don't want this night to end. The video shoot went well, I want to celebrate," Isaac suggested.

31

Cruising down 80 on their way to the country club, Isaac fired up a blunt while they jammed to Mary J. Blige's, Share My World. Jordan was having the time of her life. A few hours of drinking and trying to bowl helped her to momentarily forget what she had been through. "It's good to see you smile. You should do it more often," Isaac took a sip of his drink.

"I'm having so much fun, thank you for this," Jordan said, giving him a kiss on the cheek.

He pulled her into his embrace and replied, "No need to thank me, it's my pleasure."

Isaac realized that Jordan was loaded and decided it was time to call it a night. Of course she put up a fight, talking about she was cool until she noticed she was slurring.

Two months later...

Business had picked up for the girls, clients were rolling in. Snow had become Wayne's mistress and he paid ten thousand a month to have her all to himself. He was married, but his wife knew he was fucking around so she wasn't giving up no pussy. Red was booked with only high-end clientele. Money was flowing, each woman brought in stacks a week.

Raine and Sariya were growing too fast and wanted in on the action, but Jordan, being the big sister she was wasn't having it. Raine's eighteenth birthday was around the corner, if she still wanted to be involved with the business once she was an adult, then by all means Jordan would allow it. Alexis suggested they throw her a party for graduation and her birthday combined. Raine was excited.

Isaac agreed to perform at the event, but the ladies, still a bit nervous about possibly being found by Trent's team, wanted to keep a low profile. Jordan explained that it had to be an invitation only party.

"I'm too juiced. This party is about to go down," Raine hollered.

"You made sure to let your people know it's invitation only?" Jordan concerned.

"Yes, sis! For the last time, don't worry. Alexis hired security guard's to work the door and I know you will be strapped," Raine explained.

At nine that evening the guests started to arrive at the hall downtown that the girls rented for the evening. The D.J. was dropping hit after hit and the dance floor was filled with youngsters shaking what the Lord had blessed them with.

Saryia was a year younger than Raine but more mature. She was in a hurry to be part of the business and as she would say, "Stack my coins."

Snow seemed like the only one still trying to get revenge on Trent's team. She would sneak off to the city to spy on them and to see how they were moving. Nothing had changed, it was a full operation and it helped that they had some police on their payroll.

Staking out the place, she learned a lot about some of the men on Asad's team. For instance, Justin lived in San Leandro by the

Marina with his wife and kids. Larry lived alone in a condo in downtown Oakland.

With the money she was getting from Wayne, she had gotten an apartment in downtown Sac using an alias. The apartment was loaded with straps hidden all around the house. When she needed to get away, that was her hideout. Being raped over the years had fucked with her brain and killing was the only thing that made her feel better.

Jordan was falling in love with Isaac which concerned Alexis because that wasn't part of the plan. Not that she was trying to hate, life was finally good for them and she wanted it to stay that way. Alexis' mind was far from falling in love with any men, having her childhood ripped away from her had done some damage to her heart.

"Raine, you having fun, sis?" Jordan hollered over the music.

"You have no idea, the turn up is real," Raine replied.

Snow walked up, pulling Alexis to the side. "Sis, let me holler at you for a second."

"What's up?"

"Were getting side tracked. Now that business is booming I think it's time we pay Treasure Island a visit. I've been trailing Larry and Justin, Larry lives alone so he should be an easy target," Snow suggested.

"I'm more than ready, that whole operation gon' come tumbling down fucking with me. I was watching the news the other night and three more girls came up missing. Like damn, hoes about making money too. You don't have to keep kidnapping them and so young too," Alexis explained.

Jordan walked up, "What you two over here talking about?"

"Shit! It's time for the payback to begin," Snow suggested.

"I been thinking about that too, one by one they will fall. You think Asad will remember Raine?" Jordan asked.

"Nope. Why, what you thinking?" Snow responded.

"Were going to use her to go after Asad. I don't want to just kill him, I want to ruin his whole operation. And he love pussy."

"Yeah, but Raine isn't ready," Alexis interjected.

"She's more ready than you know. Look at sis, a few dates and training, Raine can do this. All she needs is to learn the power of that pie," Jordan reassured them.

Chapter 4

Agreeing that Sunday night they would off Larry and Justin, Snow had been following the men's routines. She knew Justin's wife and child wouldn't be home. Fatima, Justin's wife went to visit her mother out in Stockton daily. Snow took Jordan and Alexis to the hideout where she kept her straps, laughing because they too had spots in Sac just in case Trent's team found out where they lived.

"Glad to see we're all on our toes. Let's go eat Sunday dinner and then we out to the Bay," Jordan advised.

Sunday dinner consisted of beef roast with potatoes, carrots, mushrooms, rice and corn bread. Trent made sure they knew how to do everything that made a woman a good woman just in case one of the clients wanted them permanently.

Nine o'clock came around fast. Headed down 80 towards their destination, Alexis fired up a blunt and popped the patron to ease their minds. Making it to Oakland, it was still early and people were still out. Parking in the cuts, close enough to see when Larry made it in, hours went by and there was still no Larry. Snow was about ready to give up when Alexis shouted, "There he go right there!"

Jordan whispered, "Let's do this."

Placing there wigs on their heads along with gloves on their hands and making sure their pistols were loaded, each walked up to the entrance. Larry's apartment had a security gate and Snow was pissed until she noticed a security guard walking up.

Sweet talking her way into the apartments, she lied, telling him she'd just moved in and forgot her code. At first he was hesitant until she bent over, acting like she had dropped something. And bingo, they were in.

Alexis knocked on the door, "I have your delivery."

"I didn't order shit," Larry said, opening the door.

Jordan bum rushed her way in with her strapped pulled out, daring him to scream.

"Bet you didn't think you would see us again, did you?" Jordan smirked, knocking him upside his head with the pistol.

"You bitches is dumb, you should've stayed away. You not know killer Jordan, I suggest you put that heat down and go back to where been hiding."

BOOM!

Jordan hollered, "I wont do what? Say it again! Now who's the bitch?"

"What the fuck y'all want? Money? I got a hunnit stacks in my safe in my room," Larry screamed.

"Get your ass up and go get the dough before I murk your punk ass," Alexis shouted.

Crawling into the room with a bullet hole in his leg, he stumbled into his closet, opened the safe in a quick motion and turned around and let off a shot towards Alexis' head. When he missed his mark, Snow rushed in and let off three shots.

BOOM! BOOM!BOOM!

Two went into the wall, the third one landed right into his chest. Larry flew back against the wall with blood leaking from the gunshot wound. He was still breathing and tried crawling towards his pistol.

"Where the fuck you think you're going? Stupid muthafucka, you think this is about money? Money, we got. Revenge is what we're after, mark ass!" Snow yelled.

BOOM!

Jordan rushed into the kitchen and grabbed a garbage bag, filling it with the money from the safe. Heading out of the complex, she looked around to make sure no one noticed them. Jordan threw the bag filled with money in the trunk then pulled off, headed to San Leandro to take out Justin.

San Leandro was going to be a bit more dangerous, it was swarming with cops in the cuts and the neighborhood was quiet. Any noise would wake up the neighbors. Justin lived in a single family home, the lights were out, and from the looks of things Justin was in his room with the television on.

Snow was the expert in picking locks, practice would do that to a person. So many times back at the camp when Trent would lock her in the closet for talking shit, she would pick the lock and break free.

"Check y'all's straps and please remember where we are. San Leandro has a shit load of cops, so this one has to be quiet," Jordan whispered.

Finally in the house, they entered from the back door through the kitchen. The television was on full blast. Alexis, hearing movement, motioned to the other two that they had to move quickly, not giving Justin a chance to get his pistol or react to the ambush.

"You too slow, my nigga," Jordan barked as Justin tried to creep to his pistol under the sofa.

"What the fuck yall want? Get it and get the fuck out my house!" Justin yelled.

"We came for one thing," Snow yelled.

Justin looked back and forth between the three and something seemed familiar "What's that?"

"Your life! You don't recognize us do you?" Jordan smirked.

Alexis laughed, lifting up her shirt. "What about this? That's right, the three poor girls you snatched up years ago off of 90th. You had to know we were coming back for you."

"Fuck you bitches! You think you're going to murk me and get away with it? Stupid hoes!"

Snow shook her head up and down, laughing hysterically. "No, what we know is you all will fumble one by one."

POW! POW!

Running through his house looking for his stash, they stumbled on a few racks he had hidden under his mattress and hidden in some shoe boxes on top of his closet. They took those and as quickly as they could they left

Cruising onto 880 highway headed back to Sacramento, Alexis exited towards the Berkeley Marina to get rid of the evidence and the car. Jordan poured gasoline everywhere then threw in the wigs and the gloves before setting the scrapper on fire.

Hearing the police sirens from afar, each woman walked over to the rental they had tucked off near the freeway entrance. Knowing the police were going to block the roads and freeways, Snow had reserved a room at the Marriot in Emeryville.

"That shit felt too good," Snow shouted.

Alexis agreed, "Hell yeah! To have the same niggas who had been beating and raping us held at gun point is a vicious rush."

"How much did we get?" Jordan interrupted.

"Between the two we came up on $140 stacks, which is $46 and some change apiece," Alexis replied.

Changing their clothes, Alexis ordered take out and they sat back watching the news. The car was discovered, but nothing was said about the killing of Larry and Justin. After a few hours and feeling that the coast was clear, the ladies headed back home.

Driving down highway 80, Alexis asked, "How long you think it will be before they're found?"

"They both have a cleaning service come by early morning, I hope it shakes shit up at Treasure Island and Asad shits in his pants," Snow admitted.

"We have a lot more to take down before we can get to him and when we do, it will be the worst death Cali has seen," Jordan confessed.

Each girl went their separate ways once making it home. Snow had a date with Wayne and Alexis had been dating a doctor who was married. Dr. Charles Harley was a handsome, muscular African American man. He was married to his high school sweetheart and the couple had two kids.

He was dark skinned with the body of a God. Dick so big women's mouths would water at the sight of it. Charles stood five feet, nine with neat dreads that he kept freshly twisted and trimmed. For weeks he was trying to pursue Alexis, but she refused due to him being married with kids. That is until Charles offered her fifteen thousand a month to be his mistress. And that fifteen thousand came with other extravagant gifts.

For weeks they did nothing but go out on dates. Alexis wasn't ready to give him the pie just yet. She was falling for him and knew his love was off limits. Whoever his wife was, the woman was as dumb as they came. All of his time was spent with Alexis, even when the two weren't together he would blow her phone up talking about all sorts of things.

One night he'd gotten a room at the Marriot in Davis because he was horny. He was so tired to begging for it from his wife because lately she hadn't been giving it up. When he told Alexis about his wife not liking the idea of giving head and she only liked to fuck in the bedroom, Alexis laughed too hard on the inside.

Soaking in the bathtub and thinking about their first time making love had Alexis' pussy throbbing. She started to play with herself as she reminisced.

"You like what you see?" Alexis had asked Charles.

"Hell yeah. You have the fattest pussy, come here," Dr. Charles demanded.

"This is your night. You've waited long enough for this pie. Let me take off them clothes for you, I got it!" Alexis assured him.

"You sure do have it baby."

Alexis undressed Charles and lay him back on the bed. Her touch alone had his dick standing at attention. She traced his body with warm oil and gave him a deep message. The oil started to warm and make his body tingle. She put a Halls in her mouth and slowly eased the head of his dick into her mouth.

"Damn, Lexi, that shit feels to damn good," Dr. Harley mumbled.

"You like to have your dick in my mouth?"

"Yes, baby, suck that dick!" Dr. Harley slurred.

Continuing to suck his dick until he was close to exploding, she pulled it out of her mouth and blew slowly on the head. Seconds later, he started to bust. She eased his dick back in her mouth and he was trying to run. The sensation of cumming and the halls had him on one.

"I've never busted a nut like that, your mine forever," Dr. Harley insisted.

As Charles tried to catch his breath thinking the night was over, Alexis climbed on top of his face and like a homeless man he dived in like he hadn't eaten for days.

"Slow down, baby, and enjoy eating this pussy. That's it, that's how I like it. We're in no rush. It's yours, daddy, make this pussy cum for you!" Alexis moaned.

Charles did what Alexis demanded and slowed down. Alexis flipped around, positioning herself in the sixty-nine and bringing his dick back to life.

Climbing off of his face, Alexis rolled the condom on his dick with her mouth and eased him inside of her slowly. Grinding slowly as he slapped her on the ass, she bounced up and down.

"Damn, I love you, girl. This some good ass pussy! Damn, this some good as pussy!" Dr. Harley shouted.

Thinking of their time together made her bust a nut in the tub. Tonight would be there first time seeing each other since then.

Driving Snow's whip, Alexis pulled up to Old Sacramento and parked in the garage. She wasn't cool with letting the good old Doc know where she rested her head. Sitting in the car waiting for him to arrive, Alexis started to get pissed at the thought of her being stood up and texted Charles.

Alexis: If you're not here in 10 minutes I'm gone!

Placing her phone back in the Gucci bag he'd bought her on their first date, she glanced around and noticed him standing in front of a brand new Infiniti QX 80, gray on black.

"I've been waiting on you forever, I'm loving your new wheels by the way," Alexis gave Charles a hug.

Holding up the keys, Charles said, "You mean you love your new wheels. This is yours, baby! You like it?"

"Are you fucking kidding me? Do I like it? I love it!" Alexis hollered.

"I thought you would. My boy runs a dealership off of Fulton, when I saw it I thought of you."

"Wait, is this a gift like if we stop messing around you're going to take it back?" Alexis questioned.

"No, this is yours. I put it in your name and everything."

"Thank you, Charles, you have made my night! If you weren't married…" Alexis caught herself and let the sentence trail off.

Over dinner they talked about so much. Charles shared a lot about his life, Alexis shared her news about enrolling in school to get a degree in business and marketing. They were so caught up in one another that they didn't notice the woman watching them.

Looking at the two from afar, Mrs. Harley couldn't believe her eyes. There her husband was, smiling in the next woman's face like he didn't have a care in the world.

"What the fuck is this?" Kelly hollered when she walked up on them.

Charles looked up in surprise. "Kelly, what are you doing here?"

"No, Charles, the question is what are you doing? Are you cheating on me?"

"Charles, maybe we should call it a night, you know the number." Alexis walked off. Hopping in her new truck, she headed home to get Jordan so she could pick up Snow car from Old Sac. The look on his wife's face made her chuckle first and then laugh. "The power of the pie."

Jordan was at home face timing Isaac when Alexis called talking about the run in with Charles' wife. Hearing the horn honking outside, she grabbed her jacket and headed out of the door.

"Bitch, when you get this?" Jordan hollered.

Alexis grinned, "You like? Because that's the power of the pie. Charles pulled up in it at dinner, said it was a gift just because."

"I heard the fuck out of that! I guess our motto is true, there is power in the pie," Jordan chuckled.

"He been blowing my phone up since I left him to deal with his wife."

"How did he act?"

Pulling onto highway 5, she said, "Shit, he was more concerned about me than about the wife catching his ass. He been blowing me up ever since."

"Hmm, he like that pie. You must've put it on his ass."

Alexis turned into the garage, "You already know. If he wasn't married, I could see myself really messing with him."

"After tonight, he might be single real soon," Jordan acknowledged.

Chapter 5

The streets of Sacramento had become heavy with police due to the murder at IHOP. Everyone was a suspect. It was like the news reporters had nothing else to talk about and they still had no leads on the murderer.

After Raines eighteenth birthday, she convinced the older women she was ready to start putting in some work so they booked her with clients. Saying she was pretty was an understatement. She was more like drop dead gorgeous. She had the look of innocence, pure and sexy.

Raine wore her hair natural, which was big and curly. Her hazel eyes captivated any man that glanced into them. Standing five feet, four inches with a thirty-two inch waist and nice perky D cup breasts, she could have any man she set her sights on.

Jordan set up an online dating site for the girls where members were welcomed. It was her way of hiding POP Escort Service to the legal authorities. The girls were each set up with a professional photo shoot for their page. When Raine's photos uploaded to the website, higher-end clientele emerged and those type of men would definitely turn her into the woman she needed to be to spark Asad's interest. The dates would season her up a bit and lace her pockets at the same time.

Christina, Monica, and Alicia were making a little money, but not much. It was like they were outsiders, which ate them up due to them all coming from the same background. Monica believed that if they weren't going to be treated fairly, they'd have been better off left behind at Treasure Island.

POP was holding its family meeting at Sunday dinner where all of the ladies came together.

Jordan stood up. "Ladies, I would like to say good job. We have come further than I would've expected so soon. Money is flowing, but there is something me, Alexis, and Snow wanted to see if you all wanted in on. What we discuss here goes no further than this room, if you want no parts of it we will understand."

"What's wrong, J?" Raine asked.

"Red, you don't know our background and why we relocated to Sacramento. Believe us when we say if you want nothing to do with this we understand," Jordan confirmed.

Red assured them all, looking them each in the eye. "You all took me in and treated me better than my own blood. I'm rocking with POP until the end."

Jordan continued, "Glad to hear it. Years ago we all were abducted from the streets of the Bay by some men who hold an operation called Treasure Island. Being held against our will for over seven years, they did any and everything possible to break us. Anything you can think of, we went through, from rape to abuse to being sold to the highest bidder.

Raine and Sariya were kids, only eleven and ten. You would think that would've meant something to those grown ass men, but it didn't. For nights, they were molested. Finally, we built some skills on the low and got away."

Alexis cried, "Sick muthafuckas!"

Snow interjected, "It's time for payback, we got our bread up and its time to take down their whole operation one by one."

"How?" Monica asked.

"The question isn't how, the most important question is are you in or out?" Jordan asked.

Alicia hollered, "Hell yeah! Do you know how many nights I had to allow different men to fuck me? Jordan said you were there for seven years, how about me and my sisters been there for ten years plus."

"Let's do this," Sariya held up her glass.

All the ladies raised there glasses in agreement.

Jordan instructed, "First thing in the morning were off to the shooting range. You can't go to war if you can't shoot. Monica and Alicia, you're scheduled for a photo shoot right after. I know you thought we were leaving you out."

Weeks went by and everything was coming to. Going to the shooting range once a week and then off on their own in Discovery Park to shoot made them the most lethal woman in Cali. Even more so since Wayne hooked them up with heavy artillery. Niggas were gon' be shocked when they saw those women coming their way with their .45, .44 and Glock.

Since the video shoot, Isaac and Jordan hadn't been able to be separated for too long. Jordan was falling in love with Isaac. When she realized it, her mind was set on pulling back. Thinking there was no way he would want a woman like her, a woman that had slept with so many men for money, it wouldn't matter to him that it was beyond her will. On the outside all you saw was this beautiful woman, but on the inside there was so much damage.

Sitting in front of the fireplace at Isaac's home in Rancho Cordova, the two laid up under one another and watched Tyler Perry's movie Temptation. Even though she was supposed ot be enjoying herself, Jordan couldn't help but to think about the first time she was raped at Treasure Island.

It was dark by the time they made it to San Francisco and cold. Treasure Island was off to the side, close to the water. It was one of the first stops before actually making it to the city.

Alexis, Raine, and Sariya had cried the whole way there and the drivers kept yelling to them, "You bitches better shut up before I fuck you up!"

They began keeping their sighs to a minimum. Jordan hadn't shed a tear, not because she wasn't afraid, but because her father had trained her for days like that.

Jordan's father was in the military and always feared things like being kidnapped could easily happen to his child in the streets of Oakland. Teaching his young to listen to her surroundings, shooting a gun became second nature to her. They would go to the creek in Sobrante Park and let off some rounds.

The van had to have been traveling for forty minutes or so before it finally came to a stop. The driver pulled through a gate and drove straight to the back. The passenger opened the back door, leading them out one by one. When he looked at Jordan, he was quickly drawn to her, licking his lips like she was a piece of meat.

Treasure Island was built like a prison. Each girl was instructed to line up and take off their clothes. They even made the children strip naked. The passenger made his way to Jordan. Looking her up and down, he gave Trent a nod, silently informing him that he would be breaking her in.

Pulling her into a room, he immediately started taking off his clothes. Jordan just stood there looking at him like he was scum of the earth.

"Mug all you want, but I know how to wipe that shit right off," he walked over to her and socked her right in her chest like she was a nigga. Then he picked her up and did it over and over, until she fell to the floor gasping for air. Watching her crawl, trying to get out the door, he yanked her back in. "Where do you think you're going."

Throwing her onto the bed, he forced himself between her legs and started to play with her pussy. Jordan had never had sex, but she wasn't new to having her pussy played with by her high school boyfriend.

The dude was being so rough. He felt that she was only a little wet so he spit on his hand and dove into her pussy, not even caring that she was crying and blood was coming from her. The more tears he heard the harder he pumped. Jordan closed her eyes and prayed he would be finished soon. For days he kept her locked in that room, fucking her every which way, talking about he was getting her ready for the life she was about to live.

Isaac said, "Ma, you cool? You over there in deep thought, what's wrong?"

"My bad, boo. I was just thinking about Alexis' crazy ass. Sorry I zoned out."

He could sense she was lying because she wouldn't look him in the eyes. Isaac wanted them to make things official and would've been brought it to Jordan's attention but one minute she was all into him, playing the role and the next she would turn cold.

Glancing at him, Jordan thought that maybe once they shut down Treasure Island they could possibly become an item. Her grandmother told her to pray on somethings and leave it in Gods hand. Jordan decided she would do just that. She bowed her head and asked the Lord for a normal life as a wife and a mother one day.

Weeks went by before Alexis decided to forgive Charles. Tonight he was taking her to some gathering with some of his friends from back in the day. She wondered if he and his wife had ended things since Charles was taking her around friends and co-workers.

The event was being held in Davis. Alexis wore and all white silk Salvatore Ferragamo gown with a V-neck and a train flowing behind her. To top it off she wore silver Salvatore Ferragamo shoes with silver accessories.

Charles picked her up, standing there with his mouth dropped in shock at the beautiful angel that stood before his eyes. To say he was liking Alexis was an understatement, when his wife walked in on him, Charles just didn't care. Alexis made him feel things he hadn't felt in years. Yes, he should've been feeling guilty, but for years he'd tried mending the void with his wife and she hadn't put up the time and energy needed to make their marriage work.

Kelly was an old maid, a white woman. Gorgeous yes, but looks could only go so far. They had been together since college so he would always love the woman, especially since she birthed his child. She been there for him from the beginning, but from the moment he laid eyes on Alexis he was hooked like a moth to a flame.

Walking through the doors of the ballroom, everyone looked and mumbled under their breath about Dr. Charles and the woman that wasn't his wife on his arm. Alexis snickered at the old hags whose husbands' looks told that they wanted a piece of her pie. There was one particular man that caught Alexis' attention, though. His swag was old money with a mix of new money. Walking up to Dr. Charles, he asked if he could have a dance with Alexis. Charles didn't object, nor did Alexis.

"You are so gorgeous," Javier complimented.

Alexis blushed, "So are you."

"Your beauty is breathtaking. I'm leaving in tomorrow afternoon, care to have breakfast with me?" Javier asked.

"Straight to it, hun?"

"A woman like you appreciates a forward man."

Starring at him she mumbled, "Where?"

"I'm staying at the Double Tree off of Arden Way. Make sure to leave your man, or boy toy as you American woman would say, at home," Javier commanded.

Alexis was anxious to meet with Javier and to hear his story. He had body guards with him and was dipped in the finest attire. Charles was pissed that she called their date short and that she had been stingy with the pie.

Chapter 6

Back at Treasure Island...

Things had been shaken up for the crew for the first time. No woman had ever escaped, if their time was up on the island they were either sold to the highest bitter or killed. With the top hoes gone, money wasn't flowing in and to top it off someone was gunning for the crew.

Asad was paranoid, not knowing who he could trust. But he never once fathomed women taking out the crew. Someone had to have helped them escape. Losing Trent was the hardest to take in, he was his right hand man and one of the hardest men Asad had ever met.

San Francisco was holding its yearly masquerade ball, Asad and his workers always attended and tonight wouldn't be any different. Weeks after the killing of Lamar and Justin, Asad recruited more soldiers to his team. Unaware of who was gunning for his people, he was being extra careful.

Asad was far from what he appeared to be to the woman. He knew nothing about the streets, just everything on how to pimp hoes and keep them in line. He had no need to be street savvy because his line of work didn't require it.

The one thing Asad knew how to do was make money and manipulate a females. Some woman were brought to the island by force and others volunteered. Yeah, he also had his foot in the drug game. That was only because of his family already having a history in the game. Their company was well known in the streets, women would do anything to join, that is until they were trapped and saw the real get down of Treasure Island.

Asad barked, "Listen up! Tonight we need to bring in some new clients. You bitches pay haven't been up and that's not acceptable. Your ass good as dead if you come back to the island empty handed. Wait in the limo, we'll be out in a minute."

"I want everyone to be on guard tonight. As you all know were under attack, by who, I'm not sure. Anyone or anything look out of order, shoot," Asad ordered.

Asad's new right hand man, Joshua, interjected. "You know it's going to be swarming with the po-po and too many witnesses, so if you have to murk someone, do it on the low."

Pulling out of Treasure Island two stretch hummers deep, they made their way to the event. The Regency was packed with people standing out front, the media, mayor, and celebrities. Asad's drivers pulled to the front and all the cameras and lights were on them. One by one, each girl exited the car and the men whistled from the sidelines.

Jordan knew Asad like the back of her hand and she knew he would be attending the masquerade ball. Tonight was the night they had been training for. Snow copped two suits at the Regency so they would be able to do what they came for and be back in their rooms unnoticed.

Jordan cocked her .45. "Be on your toes, ladies. If Asad spots us, he wont hesitate to have one of his men take us out. We all know he gets the same table and he will have his hoes with the same get up. Tonight were not here to take him out, but to see who is new on his team. If you bump into any of his new hoes, see if you can knock'em."

"Yeah, but if the hoes seem too scary, let'em go. We don't need to be busted before shit really get popping," Alexis replied.

San Francisco weather was just right for the massacre. Two hours went by before the women went down to the ball. The party was moving. Jordan signaled for Red to come with her, she had no clue who Asad was or how he rolled.

Asad sat at his usual VIP table surrounded by women and men. The woman looked to be young and frightened. Jordan instructed Christina to lay low on top of the ballroom with her sniper just in case Asad noticed them and things went bad.

"Christina, you cool up top?" Jordan asked.

Christina whispered, "I'm cool, sis, laughing at this clown ass nigga, ready to take his ass out."

Alexis laughed, "You too?"

"Not now, it's too much fun seeing him sweat. His time will come."

"James just left the VIP, look like he heading to the bathroom," Christina glanced through her goggles.

"Monica, isn't he the one who broke you in?" Christina asked angrily.

"Been on it, you know where I'll be afterwards, ladies!" Monica walked to the men's bathroom.

Standing to the side, waiting on James to come out of the bathroom, Monica checked her pistol and made sure the silencer was on. James walked out stumbling.

Monica hollered, "Hey you! I've been watching you all night."

James turned around, grinning until he noticed the woman before him was holding a pistol.

"Not smiling anymore are you? Do you remember me?" Monica teased.

"I don't give a fuck who you are, if you gon' shoot, shoot," James barked.

Removing her mask, "It's me, Moe, the woman you molested and beat for years. Paybacks a bitch, isn't it?"

James' face held a look of shock when he really noticed the person holding the gun. With no hesitation, Monica smiled and rounded off two shots, one to the chest and one right between the eyes.

Phhtt! Phhtt!

James' body dropped to the ground, moving quickly before anyone could notice. She signaled for Alicia and the two pulled him to the exit close to the bathroom. They Dragged him out and off to the side behind a bush. They were back inside before anyone noticed that murder had just been committed.

Christina muttered, "One down and hella more to go."

Asad didn't allow his girls to wonder off too far, so rescuing a few was off limits for the night. Christina signaled Raine, it was her turn to put Asad to the test. Asad stood at the bar looking good as shit. Six feet, three, chocolate, muscles so on point they protruded through his dress shirt, his smile alone made soaked panties. He resembled the rapper 50 Cent.

If only he wasn't such a snake, Raine thought. Walking up to the bar, she ordered a Margarita, standing to the side of Asad who was ordering a few more bottles for his table.

Asad turned towards Raine, "Parton me, but your breathtaking."

"Does that line work on all the women," Raine shot back.

"I wouldn't know as women usually approach me. I'm Asad, by the way. And you are?" Asad extended his hand.

Raine returned the handshake, smiling. "I'm Zariya, my friends call me Ri."

"Nice to meet you Zariya. Am I being too forward if I ask for your number?" Asad asked.

"I'm not big on giving strangers my number and I am new to Cali, but I'll take yours, though" Raine replied.

Pulling out her burner, she plugged his phone number in and told him she would hit'em in the morning. Jordan smiled because Asad had taken the bait.

The morning of the masquerade ball…

Making it to the Marriot early to scope out the place before her date with Javier, Alexis noticed the restaurant was empty. She had Jordan come, which was protocol for POP when meeting new clientele. Thirty minutes later, Javier was escorted in with his body guards, looking so sexy. Even in the morning he was swagged out, simple but elegant in his 7 For All Mankind jeans with a button up shirt and Gucci loafers.

"Good morning, Miss Alexis. I'm honored you could join me," Javier kissed hher hand as he sat.

"Thanks for having me. Is it me or is this restaurant empty?" Alexis replied.

"Why, of course is empty, only the best for you. I noticed you came with a friend, you can assure her you're in the best hands and then we can continue."

Alexis walked over to Jordan, "I got it from here, sis."

"Okay, I'll be at the mall shopping if you need me," Jordan assured her.

"So, Mr. Javier, tell me about yourself?"

Javier sipped on his coffee, "I come from a big family with major power as you would say in your country. I'm in the pharmaceutical business, I'm on business and now pleasure."

"Pharmaceutical? Hun, so you're a doctor or pharmacist?" Alexis repeated.

"You seemed bothered, what is it? Be honest with me, Alexis."

"Truthfully, I didn't know a pharmacist could afford Salvatore Ferragamo," Alexis said.

Javier laughed at her. "You're thinking of the wrong kind of pharmacist, I'm the biggest distributer in America. It snows every day of the year because of me."

"Oh, I get it now. Are you single? Married? Have children?" Alexis caught on.

"Yes, I am single. No children as of yet, but one day. Tell me about you?" Javier responded.

Alexis paused before she replied, "Something happened to me at a young age that I'm still trying to get past. At the moment I'm trying to get a little revenge. Taking it day to day, just trying to make it."

"Sorry to see the sadness in your eyes. If there's anything I could do to keep that smile shinning and that heart happy, please allow me."

"Thanks, but I am a woman that wants to be able to make myself happy rather than rely on anyone. So how does a woman like myself get involved with your business?" Alexis asked.

"You don't want no parts of this life. Yes, it's a lot of money, but also more problems than you can think."

"Shouldn't I be the judge of that? Javier, forgive me when I say I have been to hell and back but still standing. I doubt there's much me and my team can't do. So again I ask you, how do I get into that type of business?"

"You first need a solid team, then you need somewhere to deal, as the hood would call it a trap house. And most importantly you need some soldiers who's willing to die for you. What's the saying? More money more problems? I can give you a few keys on credit and see how you do, then we can talk business," Javier advised.

"How much is a key?" Alexis asked.

Alexis already knew how much they were selling for due to the transaction she had with Makai.

"I usually let them go for twenty-two grand a key. For you, the first ten will be seventeen-five."

Alexis did the math in her head. They could get off more than that in a week with the right connections and with the clientele coming into POP, it wouldn't be hard at all.

"When did you say your flight leaves?" Alexis asked.

"Late this afternoon, but I didn't ask you to lunch to talk business. Let's first enjoy breakfast. And if you decide, let's say a week from now you want in, then we will talk business the right way."

"Will doing business affect us?" Alexis worried.

"I could never see my lady in the streets slanging. She would have to work for nothing. I've never met a woman like yourself so I may bend the rules."

The two continued with breakfast and no longer discussed business. Javier loved how she was great with conversation and hated the fact that she wanted in on business. It was against family business to date within the organization.

Alexis hugged Javier, "Breakfast was great and I look forward to hearing from you. Too bad you have to leave so soon. Until next time."

Chapter 7

Asad was furious, no one could find James. Last time he was seen was when he went to the restroom at the masquerade ball. Thinking about the woman he met at the party had him smiling just a bit. He had yet to meet a woman who could turn him down.

Zariya, was gorgeous. They had been texting since the ball, nothing major, just getting to know one another. He asked her for a night cap, but she refused. Raine went on, telling him how she wasn't that type of girl and asked if women really fell for that hooking up with a man they barely knew mess.

He replied, "You would be surprised!"

And to his reaction she shot back, "There are too many kidnappers and molesters out there to just go out with someone you don't know."

Asad knew exactly what she was referring to because he ran a company where eighty percent of the women were kidnapped and raped.

Asad ended the text messages with, "Good night beautiful and sleep tight."

The girls were reading the text messages out loud as they were on their way back home, dying laughing at that nigga.

Waking up the next morning, Alexis called an emergency meeting with Snow and Jordan to be held at IHOP.

"Something must be real important that we had to hold a meeting outside the house," Snow yawned.

Alexis had been anxious to tell them about her date/meeting with Javier since they'd made it home the night before. She took a drive through Natomas and came upon a perfect location to set up trap houses. There were a few younger dudes that were slanging nickel and dime pieces, but not getting any dough.

Alexis whispered, "Yesterday I met up with that cute Cuban and came up on some information I think can take us to the next level."

"Stop talking in circles and spit it out," Jordan said with a slight attitude.

Alexis smirked. "His family is big time, they distribute the best cocaine in the US that money can buy."

"So what are you really trying to suggest?" Snow asked.

"We should get into that business. Javier said he'd drop the price to seventeen-five where we can sell them for at least twenty-five stacks, plus set up a few trap houses. I already been scouting out the perfect location off of W. El Camino. They have apartments over there with knocks running all through there," Alexis said.

"I bypass there all the time, some youngsters are slanging out there," Jordan replied.

Alexis nodded her head in agreement. "They're not a part of no organization, small time, not making no dough. Either they're with us or against us."

"We can't think these men are going to just let us take over their spot," Snow look at Alexis like she had lost her mind.

"Let us? We don't need anyone to let us do shit, our gun play is official. This what we do, buy a few keys from Javier, approach the dudes in the apartment complex on some joining the team hype. If they object, it's lights out and we taking over by force. I'll hit Makai up about breaking down the work because we don't know shit on how to cook up no dope, " Jordan explained.

Alexis cheezed, "That's what the fuck I'm talking about. Snow, you down?"

"Hell yeah, we have to tell the crew and we should let nocks sample the product so word can get out. And we already know some cops that work the area, might have to hit'em off with some dough to look the other way," Snow suggested.

Monday's were slow nights for POP. In the house, everyone was maxing and relaxing, watching Love and Hip Hop. The shit these hoes did for the extra attention was stupid.

Going in front of the television, Snow asked for an emergency meeting. "Sorry to interrupt the show, but we have important business to discuss. What do you all think about going into the drug business?"

Christina chimed in, "I don't know about that. These niggas gone feel some type of way with us stepping into their territory."

"Chris, since when do we bow down to a nigga? Them days are over for each of us in this room, our gunplay speaks for itself. We have a connect willing to give a good deal, the location has already been picked," Jordan said.

"If you're in, raise your hands. If out, we'll understand. You can just continue working up under POP." Alexis took a vote and each hand went up.

Jordan barked, cocking her gun. "First things first, ladies. Strap up, it's time we make our presents known. The location we're about to take over is ran by some youngster who go by the name Jack. He has two options, jump on board or meet his maker."

Posted up between the apartments, they were setting up shop, waiting for the target to show his face. Alexis paged him for some blow and Jack said he would meet her at Bel-Air.

Jack walked with his hoodie over his head, heading to bust this knock talking about spending some money. He needed all the dough he could get, nickel and diming wasn't paying the bills. His rent was seven days late and he was the sole provider for his little sister.

"Jack? Over here," Alexis whispered.

Jack was hesitant to walk over. Once seeing she wasn't alone, he did a quick turnaround but was caught off guard by five gorgeous woman blocking his path.

"Excuse me, ladies," Jack gestured, trying to walk past.

Jordan stood in front of him. "How are you, Jack? I'm, J, these are my sisters, Red, Alexis, Snow, Christina and Monica. We noticed you slang in these parts and had a business proposition for you."

"You must have me confused with another Jack."

Alexis explained, "Jack, like my sister was saying, we see you struggling out here in these streets. I know selling nickel bags can't be taking care of you and your sister. What would you say if I told you that getting down with us could easily make you ten stacks a week, maybe even more?"

"By doing what?" Jack asked.

"Get down with the team. Don't get us wrong, we're taking over with or without your help, but out of respect were giving you away in. Think about our proposal, we'll give you until the morning. Have a safe night, Jack," Monica recommended.

Jack walked off, headed back to his apartment to ponder his decision. Part of him felt insulted by being threatened by some bitches. How you gon' roll up on me with some get down or lay down bullshit? But ten stacks a week would have him living right. And the bitch, J, say that would only be the beginning. What he could do with that kind of dough... It was final, if those bitches had the balls to step to him, they had what it took for the game. He was in.

Not wasting time with getting things ready to make the move, Alexis found three apartments available in each complex. The next morning when she headed out to pay for each, the management thought she had lost it. But once they ran her credit and saw it was excellent, she was able to get the keys to each unit and pay for the rent for months in advance.

After getting the keys to the units, Alexis went back to the house to pick up Jordan and Monica so they could go over to Home Depot off of Truxel.

"What we getting from here?" Monica asked.

"Three steel doors for the units. Sensor lights and something to lock each window," Alexis explained.

Monica smiled, "This bitch not playing."

"The apartments will only be the trap houses and they will only hold so much product. We need a stash house just in case we have to shake if po-po come knocking," Jordan recommended.

"Great minds think alike. I found a house across the street for sale. Contact the realtor and the fiends can't know about it, this is our secret hideout to watch what's going on or escape."

Alexis stood in line, feeling her phone vibrate. She reached in her Gucci bag and read the text.

Text: I'm in, just let me know what's the next move.

Jack was in, which made the girls feel better about the move. If they had to kill him, then so be it. Alexis made the call to Javier, they scheduled a meeting that weekend to go over business.

Days went by and Alexis was beyond anxious to get business rolling, but she was also anxious to also see Javier. There was something about that man that made her pussy wet. As a reward, Jordan shot Jack a few stacks for joining the team and to move him and his sister somewhere away from the trap.

In downtown Sac, Dr. Harley was glancing out of his window thinking about how he was going to make Alexis his permanently. Ever since his wife busted in on them, she wasn't feeling the mistress role any longer. His wife wanted out of the marriage, not because he was cheating, but because he just didn't give a fuck about their marriage anymore.

The knock at the door broke Charles out of his daydreaming. Then in walked his receptionist letting him know he had a visitor. To his surprise it was Alexis, bringing him Starbucks and a bagel to get his day started.

He blushed and escorted her inside his office, "I was just thinking about you, surprised to see you."

"I can see, been so busy lately and I didn't want you to think I had forgot about you," Alexis replied.

Charles' smile grew brighter. "I actually did for a second, but you're here now so we can put that behind us and move forward."

Alexis shook her head, "I'm here to tell you that I can't continue this, us, we have to end. One day I want to be someone's wife and you're not an option for me."

"Why not?"

Alexis chuckled, "What do you mean why not? Your married, Charles, in case you forgot."

"I'll file for divorce!" Charles was dead serious.

"I can't ask you to do that," Alexis scolded.

Charles walked around his desk. "You don't have to, my marriage has been over for years. We were just holding on for the kids."

"Take your time and really think about this. I'm not in the position to be in a relationship right now, I have so much going on. Friends we can stay, and if down the line you're single and things have settled in my life, we can take it from there," Alexis advise.

Charles replied, "I guess, I have no choice but to understand. Just promise me you wont disappear again and we can still date?"

"Sure."

The life she had didn't lead her into the path of a wife or girlfriend of a doctor, but maybe down the line.

Makai came down to help them put together the trap house and teach them how to cook the ya-yo. Jordan felt it was important that each knew how, just in case something went all bad and workers had to be replaced.

Tonight was the long drive down to San Diego to meet up with Javier and his dad. They wanted to get a feel of the women and their set up. After weeks of pondering how they would transport the keys, Snow came up with the perfect set up. They opened up a small car lot and would be transporting the drugs in the cars from the car auctions.

Pulling into the airport in San Diego, Snow, Jordan, and Alexis caught a shuttle over to Hertz Rental Car and picked up a rental and then headed over to the hotel to change before their meeting. Changing into some clothes that said sexy but also not to fuck with them, they had to meet up with a dude Wayne had hooked them up with for some straps.

"You ladies ready?" Jordan asked, strapping her piece up under skirt.

Alexis replied, "Born ready."

Going into the Restaurant, they found that it was empty. Javier and his team were seated around a table as his security guard stopped the women and patted them down. The security took away all of their weapons, all except for Jordan's because she had it tucked away.

"Ladies, we finally meet," Ivian, Javier's father said.

"Nice to finally meet you," Alexis shook his hand firmly and looked him in his eyes.

"You women are too beautiful. Please have a seat and order something, this is the best restaurant in San Diego," Ivian explained.

Placing their orders, Jordan was anxious to get down to business. However, she was patient, not wanting to show any disrespect. After eating and having a few drinks, Jordan said, "Ivian, if we can please, let's get down to business."

Ivian smiled, he knew she would be the savvy one by her appearance. "How many you think you can push in a week and how do you plan on transporting?"

"We opened up a small used car lot. The ladies will be tucked away upon delivery of the vehicle, we were thinking twenty-five keys a week to start and if business picks up we will discuss more," Alexis responded.

"If you can up it to, let's say thirty keys a week, I'll lower the tag on the kids to, let's say fifteen-five a key," Ivian shot back.

Snow interjected, "You have a deal. W'ell be ready for our first shipment in a few days and will also have your money."

Javier raised his glass, "Let's make a toast to new business."

Everyone around the table raised there glasses and made the toast. The deal had been sealed and it was time to take things to a new level for POP.

Chapter 8

Two weeks later…

Word traveled fast in Sacramento about the product POP was pushing. At first selling 30 keys was a challenge until the fiends started coming through in bolts. Jordan fronted Jack five keys to sell, giving him ten percent off top for whole selling and a flat amount on anything broken down.

Christina and Monica ran one trap house, in a few weeks' time they had recruited their own soldiers to post outside. In the beginning the guys were hesitant to be part of a crew that was run by women but in due time Jack became more like family then a worker.

On Sundays he and his sister would join POP for Sunday dinner. How he looked at it, he was blessed to have them come into his life. As a result, he finally able to pay the bills on time and taking care of his sister made him feel like a man.

Back at Treasure Island, Asad's team started fumbling. Money was tight and hoes were trying to escape on what seemed like every day. No one made it past the gate and to punish them for trying to leave, Asad made them go days without eating.

There was still no word on what had happened to James. The news said they found his body outside of the hotel with two bullet wounds, one to the head and one to his chest. He and Zariya talked via text every day. She had yet to agree to going out with him, but little by little she was giving in. Something about Zariya was intriguing, he didn't know if it was her playing hard to get or the simple fact she could hold a descent conversation.

Asad called Zariya, "Hey boo, what you up to?"

"Hey, Asad. Nothing much, just leaving the hair salon now, on my way to do a little retail therapy."

"Can I come?" Asad asked.

"Umm, sure. Let's meet up in Vacaville at the outlets, let's say four?" Raine replied.

Asad was excited to finally be able to see her again. "Hell yeah."

Four o' clock came around fast. Raine had decided to wear something simple, a pair of blue True Religions, some tan Ugg's, and a tan blazer. She had her beautician add some blonde highlights to her hair and chop her up some heavy layers to frame the front of her face.

The weather in Vacaville was gloomy, looked like rain was coming in soon. Waiting outside in front of the outlets for him to pull up, Raine got a little nervous, hoping Asad didn't recognize her. Seeing him pull up in his black Tahoe, she did a double check to ensure she had her piece.

Strolling up, grinning, Asad said, "You are too gorgeous."

"Why, thank you. You're quite handsome yourself, shall we spend our hard earned money?" Raine walked towards the 7 For All Mankind store.

Hours went by and each time Raine would try to pull out her wallet to pay for her things, Asad would put her hand away and pull out his black card. Once she realized he was fronting the bill on the shopping spree, she went into all the high end stores. Three thousand into his pockets and she finally thought it was time to call it a day.

"You didn't have to pay for my clothes. I work hard for my money, I can afford to splurge," Raine mumbled.

Asad put her bags in her trunk, "I'm quite sure you could, but I wanted to treat you. Maybe down the line you could do the same for me."

Glancing at him, she had to admit the man was fine. Standing six feet, three, smooth chocolate complexion, body looking right, always clean cut and his eyes were light brown and to die for. She thought, If only you weren't such a snake, the possibilities...

"Zariya are you listening to anything I just said?"

"I'm sorry, I was daydreaming. What were you saying?" Raine asked.

"I was asking if you wanted to grab something to eat."

"Sure, where do you want to go?"

Asad replied, "Outback Steakhouse don't sound too bad."

Following him to the restaurant, Raine called Jordan, letting her know things were good and that she was on her way to dinner with Asad. Later into the meal Asad started asking all kind of questions, trying to get to know her more. Raine had prepared herself for everything he asked and replied without any hesitation. He didn't hesitate on telling her about his life, but not once did he reveal he ran Treasure Island, was a kidnapper, and was child molester.

"Dinner was great, we have to do this again sometime," Raine stood.

Asad replied as they walked out of the restaurant to her car, "That we do, when can I see you again?"

"Whenever is good with me," Raine assured him.

Raine gave Asad a hug and a kiss on the cheekk before heading down 80 towards Sac. She rode around the city for an additional thirty minutes making sure he hadn't followed her.

Business was running good, too good for some people in Sac. The niggas in South Sac weren't feeling the new cats coming to their city and taking over. Their price and product was out ranking the shit Maricio was pushing. Maricio was distributor in South Sacramento, one well talked about drug dealers. He tried to send some of his goons to the North to see who was running the operation, but they came back with nothing.

Where they were slanging from, he knew a youngster who used to hustle, but nothing major. Hopping in his Escalade, he took a ride through Natomas. Seeing Jack standing outside chopping it up with some youngsters, he pulled up, hollering his name.

Talking to his crew to see how much work they had left, Jack's back was turned when the truck pulled up. Hearing his name being called, he turned around and noticed it was Maricio from the South side. Maricio was this ugly, fat, black dude who tried using his weight to intimidate people. Jack wasn't surprised, he knew the day would come sooner or later.

"What's good, Maricio?" Jack asked.

"Shit, you tell me, you big time now. How that happen overnight?" Maricio replied.

"Why you worried about what's going on this way?" Jack barked.

Maricio shook his head. "You taking from my plate so I got a problem with that."

"I don't give a fuck what you got a problem with, you come roll through my shit and think you about to shut down what's cracking over here. I advise you to take your ass back to the south and figure out what you need to do to stay on top," Jack barked.

With a head nod Maricio said, "I'll be seeing you in the streets."

"Nigga, is that a threat? We can handle this right now, no need to wait. I'm telling you, Maricio, you don't want this kind of beef, you will lose. So I'll advise you to keep it pushing," Jack barked.

Pulling off, Maricio was beyond pissed. That young nigga must have forgotten who the fuck he was, talking about he didn't want

78

his kind of beef. It was time to get them thangs cracking because there couldn't be two kings in Sac. It wasn't big enough.

In a few weeks time, Jacks crew had already knocked three of his main buyers. There was no way Jack came up that fast with somebody else not fronting the bill. He could talk all that big shit, but Maricio was about to wreak havoc on anyone who was involved and then take over Natomas.

Jack went to holler at the crew about Maricio and informed them that a war between the two spots would soon break out.

"How deep is this dude in the south?" Jordan asked.

Jack hit the Hennessey bottle, "He has a squad, but only two. We have to worry about his main hitters. Maricio supplies the south side."

Jordan barked, "See if we can persuade some of his people to join the team, offer them more than what they getting from him. We also need some more soldiers, some that's money hungry and not afraid to get dirty. Start recruiting."

Going on a date with Isaac was just what Jordan needed to get her mind off of the fact that she was beefing with some nigga over turfs. She and Isaac hadn't made it official, not that he didn't want to. He'd been pressuring her for the past few weeks on making things final and living with each other. Of course she couldn't take on a relationship, Isaac thought he knew the woman sitting before him, but he only knew so much.

Yes, Jordan cared for him, at times she thought maybe there was love and if in time things grew, so be it. But as of now, her only focus was rising to the top, stacking her coins and taking out Treasure Island. Jordan was infatuated with the power hustling gave her and killing had become second nature.

"Are you enjoying your meal, boo?" Isaac asked.

"Am I, this is too good. You know I love me some seafood. What's next on our agenda?"

"Desert," Isaac grinned.

"You so nasty," Jordan laughed.

"We been talking for what, three months now? When are we going to make this official?"

"Isaac, I told you I'm not ready for a relationship. What's wrong with just dating and seeing where this can take us?" Jordan cooed.

"I don't want to just be your friend, I'm trying to be your man. I can have any woman I want, I'm choosing you and you're turning me down."

"I want you too, but there's too many things I need to be focused on and there's still so much you still don't know about me."

"Then tell me. Stop bottling up your emotions and let me in, you can trust me."

"I will one day, I'm just not ready to talk about it yet," Jordan explained.

"J, I'm going on tour for a few weeks. I hope by then you're ready because if not, I'm moving on."

Jordan stood to leave, "You're sitting here giving me a time frame to commit and if I don't you're moving on? Then that's what you should do because I wont be forced into something I'm not ready for. All I asked you for was a little more time."

Jordan got up from the table and called Alexis to pick her up. As she walked a few blocks away from the restaurant, the tears began to flood. Honestly, she didn't know what she wanted. There she was with a man wanting to make her his woman and it wasn't enough. Isaac wasn't any man either, he was one of the biggest rappers known. He had money, power and brains.

Chapter 9

POP had grown deep throughout Sac. The group recruited a big majority of Maricio's squad yet nothing had popped off as of yet. Jack knew better, though, he knew Maricio was waiting for the right time to strike.

Money was flowing on both sides of the company, po-po had been coming through deeper than usual so Jordan hired more Sac authorities preparing for a war between the two turfs. Detective Brown was on payroll and informed Jordan that shit was about to hit the fan and that they keep a low profile.

Jordan wasn't feeling that. If Maricio wanted to take them down, she wasn't waiting around to see. Taking a threat lightly could cause her to lose someone in the organization.

Christina and Monica were waiting for the shipment at the dealership, the truck was taking longer than usual. Glancing out front, Monica noticed it pulling to the side of the building with ten other cars. Opening up the gate to let them in, they started to unload the order.

Monica was trying to hurry shit up, something didn't seem right and she wanted to send the truck on its way. They spent thirty minutes unloading the cars on the lot, securing the packages, and stashing the keys in hidden compartments at the dealership.

Walking to the car to head to the trap house, Monica said, "I felt uneasy about tonight, I'm too happy that shit went cool."

"Yeah, me too. For some reason I been feeling like someone has been watching us," Christina said, unlocking the car.

A black Buick pulled up as the women were talking, neither noticed until bullets started flying.

BOOM! BOOM!

Monica screamed, "Bitch, get down! Aww, shit."

Christina ducked behind the door and pulled out her strap, shooting it in the direction of the car. Once the car was out of sight, they both hoped in their own car and pulled off.

"Where is that blood coming from?" Monica asked.

Christina looked down and noticed she had been shot in her arm. Blood was gushing out, "Oh shit, I've been hit! Take me to the hospital."

Monica urged, "Go back to the parking lot and we'll call the police. But first we have to get Jack to come move the keys."

Chilling at the Country Club off of Watt Ave with some of his crew and his little bop, Jack was hanging, trying to clear his head. Feeling his phone vibrate, he looked at the message.

Text: Code 911, 2021-1.

That was code to hurry to the dealership alone. Rushing to his truck, he checked his pistol and was on his way down Watt. When he got there, Monica and Christina were out front. Hopping out of the car, he noticed blood on Christina.

"What the fuck happened?" Jack barked.

"I've been shot, we can go into details later. Clear the kids so I can call them boys to go to the hospital."

After dialing a few numbers, some people showed up and Christina was immediately taken to an underground hospital. It was a secret spot located in Sac that only those who were on the other side of the law knew about.

Being in the business they were in, that ladies all knew that if anything ever popped off and any of them got hurt, a regular hospital was out of the question. Not only would going there put them at risk of being exposed, it could also put them in the spotlight and that spotlight could lead Asad right to them. So for some extra change, they got the info they needed and got themselves added to the list of VIP's that would be taken to the undisclosed medical facility when bullets and bloodshed came into play.

The Dr. there was the best in the business and Christina knew that she would be well taken care of. Monica stayed with Christina while Jack took the keys to their second hiding spot, they one they bought in case shit like that happened.

Maricio had made his move and it was time to take him and his crew out. POP was prepared. Taking his men was a move made because they were going to expand on the south side after taking Maricio out. Regardless of how many years he had been in the game, he wasn't the smartest hustler around.

POP was making their move on him and his crew right up under their nose. Raine and a few other girls had been dating some of Maricio's men for the last few weeks. Tonight he was hosting a fight party as a cover up for his whereabouts when the shooting occured just in case anyone tried to snitch on him.

Raine excused herself to the ladies room. Checking her phone, Monica let her know that Chirstina was hit. Unlocking the front door for Jack, Monica, Alicia, and Raine rejoined the party. It was now or never, time to make their move. Shooting Christina forced them to retaliate sooner than expected.

Jack busted in hollering, "All you niggas get the fuck down!"

"What the fuck?" Maricio replied.

"Nigga, did I stutter? Drop to your knees," Jack barked.

As Jack checked his surroundings, a bit shaken up, Maricio tried to go for his gun. But Jordan pulled out her strap and yelled, "Nigga, I wish you would! Lay your fat ass down."

"You hoes set us up," Maricio's worker hollered.

"You should've kept your fat ass on this side of town and collected your coins. But no, you wanted beef and shot my sister," Jordan said.

Maricio spit, "You bitches ain't got the balls to shoot."

POW! POW!

Alicia shot Maricio's friend in the head and chest. "No, we got the pussy that made you dumb muthafuckas think with your dicks and get caught slipping."

"Jack, you sitting here allowing some bitches to run you? We both know you don't have the balls, you a mark. Has been and always will be," Maricio challenged.

BOOM! BOOM!

Jack shot Maricio in the chest and his body flew back into the couch. He was still breathing, coughing up blood, until Jack walked up to him and put two more shots to his chest.

Raine called the clean-up crew, "I want to place an order. Four orders to go in forty-five minutes."

When it was all said and done, looking around Maricio's trap house, no one would have believed anyone was murdered. The clean-up crew did a great job and then they dumped the bodies.

Detective John worked South Sacramento and he knew something wasn't right. No one was out on Maricio's corners and none of his crew had been seen. His sergeant had been on the whole department about the blood shed lately in Sac and the people turning up missing.

Whoever was taking over was smart. No evidence was ever left behind and there were never any witnesses. Tthat's what pissed detective John off more. His meal ticket had been taken away and whoever had anything to do with it was gon' break bread or get locked up.

An emergency meeting was called a week after the killing of Maricio just to make sure people were cool and knew what their roles were. Shit had finally died down in the South, Alexis thought it was a good idea to set up shop with the workers they'd recruited from Maricio. At first Snow was skeptical about the idea because if they crossed Maricio, they could do the same to them.

"I'm glad to see everyone could make it. Christina is doing much better and will be released from the hospital in a few days. We have decided to let Eric run the corners in the South with three other workers," Jordan said.

Jack interrupted, "Do you think that's a good idea? Shit is hot, the po-po looking for the shooters and from what I hear Detective John been asking around about us."

"Who's Detective John?" Alexis asked.

"He was on Maricio's team and he isn't happy that his meal ticket was knocked off."

Eric suggested, "It's simple, we add him to our payroll. We need some of them boys in the South on our team anyway."

Jordan shook her head, agreeing. "Smart thinking, Eric. Monica will do the cooking along with Sariya. We need a few locations, one for the yayo and the other for the money. I don't want the money in the same location as the kids."

With being hit, something was needed to lift everyone out of there funk. The girls thought it was a good idea to take everyone out to turn up and celebrate their come up and their first encounter with the streets. It wouldn't be their last, though. This was just the beginning because with more money came more problems.

Jordan was just going through the motions. Isaac hadn't been kidding when he's given her the ultimatum. She tried calling him, asking for more time and trying to invite him to the event they were throwing on New Year's Eve. After days of trying to reach him with no success, she gave up.

Tonight was the night. They'd hired some promoters to advertise the event on the radio, on social media and in commercials. Local artist were coming out to perform, a few from the Bay, E-40, Too Short, Danny from Sobrante and some others.

Snow was a bit skeptical about the event, people from surrounding cities were coming which could've meant Asad and his crew. The women were all getting ready for the night, music was blasting from the living room surround sound, bottles were already cracked open.

Raine walked through the hall dressed in a bad ass light pink dress with gold accessories screaming, "Turn down for what!"

"This bitch already on one," Sariya said.

"Damn, baby, can I get your number?" Jordan walked out strutting towards Raine.

By ten-thirty the party bus had arrived and the girls were headed out. As they rode, they passed blunts and swooped up Jack, Eric and Lamont. Jack was looking too good rocking an all-black Armani suit with some black Salvatore Ferragamo shoes.

Alicia hadn't told anyone, but she was feeling him to the tee. They'd spent most of their days together in the trap houses talking about everything. He'd never made a pass at her so she figured he wasn't interested, that is until he came on the bus, sat right beside her and kiss her on the cheek. "You look gorgeous, my queen."

Alicia blushed. "So do you, my king."

Pulling up to the Hilton, the parking lot was swarming with people. Jack questioned why the women didn't want to go through the front. Seeing the hesitation in their response, he just dropped it.

Music was blasting and the performers were tearing the stage up. Jack was having the time of his life. For the first time ever people respected him and his pockets was filled with money. Females who never paid him any mind when he was selling nickel bags, slanging on the block, were now throwing their panties at him. All he did was chuckle and laugh in their faces. The only thing he would use them for was a nut.

Those hoes weren't loyal, all they saw were dollar signs and a way out the hood. Jack respected Jordan and her crew, they were some ruthless women. But by looking at them, you couldn't tell.

Being a witness to their gunplay, he knew better than to get on their bad side. He had eyes for one in the crew, but didn't know how he felt about fucking around with someone he slanged with because if shit didn't go right between the two it could fuck up his money.

Alicia had been showing signs that she wanted to be down and tonight verified she wanted more from their friendship. Shorty was bad and knew her shit in the streets, one of the best cookers in the crew. Alicia could cook up a key, break it down and have it out in the streets in a few hours' time. Sitting back in the VIP, Jack allowed her to act as his woman. How could he complain? She had been giving him lap dances all night, throwing the kitty at him.

"Bruh, you over there getting the VIP treatment, let me find out you scared," Jordan laughed.

"Yeah right, I'm just chilling," Jack replied.

Alicia jumped in, "He scared, sis."

For the first few hours the party was cool, no drama. Snow alerted the ladies that Asad was in the building looking more like it was for pleasure than for business. Some were pissed because they would have to stay in VIP for the night. He would for sure notice them and fuck up their plan.

Since the masquerade ball, nothing else had been done to The Treasure Island crew. Raine was working her magic and had Asad hooked and he hadn't even hit it yet. Seeing him smiling and all happy and shit pissed Snow off, she wanted to take his ass out. Of course Jordan wasn't haven't it. Sac was now their place of business so making shit hot wasn't an option.

"You not gon' believe who just walked in the door looking hot as fuck!" Red yelled.

"Who?" Jordan asked.

"Just wait, you'll see," Red smiled.

Scanning the room to see who the hell Red was talking about, she spotted him. Isaac was looking too good, but he wasn't alone. He came with some thot on his arm. Jordan had been the woman that she was so she just nodded her head and looked away. Was she hurt? Fuck yeah! But he would have to come better than flaunting a bitch rocking Walmart gear.

"That bitch look dumb," Alexis said.

"That she do. What is that in her hair?" Sariya replied.

Cracking jokes, the ladies hadn't noticed Isaac walk up with his chick. "Hello, ladies, Jordan?"

"What's up, Isaac? When you get back in town?" Jordan questioned.

Isaac was getting pissed off about her nonchalant reaction. "A few days now. I wanted to introduce you to my girl. Jasmine, this is Jordan, one of my good friends."

Jasmine grinned, "Nice to meet you, Jordan. This VIP is off the hook and you rocking that Prada dress, girl."

Jordan got up and smirked. "That, I am! Thank you, Jasmine, you two have a good night. And Isaac, I think she is the one."

Walking away pissed, Isaac thought bringing Jasmine to the event would piss Jordan off. It didn't piss her off, but it did something he would later regret.

Chapter 10

None of the girls knew it, but Raine was feeling Asad. The only thing that kept her from falling too hard was her knowing his background. He walked in the party like he owned it. Once he spotted her, he treated her like a queen.

Asad was sporting nothing but Gucci from head to toe with some Gucci Guilty cologne. His hair freshly cut, dipping with waves. His jewelry game was on point as he rocked a custom made Gucci watch with green and red diamonds tracing around.

All night the two were cuddle up, the smell of his cologne alone had Raine's pussy wet. Tonight was going to be the night she gave in and introduced him to the best pie money could buy.

"You spending the night with me?" Asad bent down and whispered in her ear.

Raine looked into his eyes. "I don't know if I'm ready for that."

"Just let me hold you, seems like you're always running."

Raine looked down, debating. "Sure, why not? You did drive all the way down here to spend time with me. It's the least I can do."

Going to the back where the dressing rooms were, one of Asad's workers thought he saw Monica going to the ladies room. He was loaded so he thought maybe he was tripping. Standing outside of the door, he waited for her to come out. A woman exited and walked past him, glancing at him like he'd lost his mind. She walked out and bumped into Omar, "Excuse me, Monica?"

Monica looked up from her purse, "I don't think I know you."

"You know me alright, I took your virginity. Wait until I tell Asad you been hiding out in Sac town." Omar pulled Monica by the arm.

Fear of going back to Treasure Island went through her head as he pulled her away from the hall where the restrooms were. Going into her purse, she pulled out her .38 and yanked away from Omar, yelling "I'm not going no damn where with you, you fucking sleaze ball! Turn your molesting ass around!"

Doing as he was told, he staggered into Too Short's dressing room. Out of all of the times for it to be empty, now wasn't that time "Come on, Monica, you don't have to do this. Just let me go and I won't tell Asad shit."

"Muthafucka, did you forget you molested me for years? Let you go?" Monica laughed like a maniac and locked the dressing room door. Looking at the fear in Omar eyes made her feel a bit at ease until she reflected on the first time he molested her.

She was only sixteen years old, out in San Leandro, leaving the after school program. It was early, but the sun had already gone down. She walked towards Bay Fair, so she could get home. A raggedy Buick went past her and bust a quick U-turn. Before Monica had a chance to react, two men jumped out and shoved her in the trunk. She screamed and hollered for help, but no one paid any attention. To shut her up, Omar hit her so hard that she passed out.

She'd been awakened by ice cold water and men just gawking at her. Monica begged and pleaded for them to let her go. Looking down at her, laughing like she had just told a joke, the men walked out. All but Omar. He yanked her up off of the floor and stripped her down. Her body was only so strong, she was a young fragile teenager.

Standing in the nude, afraid to move or speak, she just stood there and looked at the man before her undress. Pushing her down to the bed, Omar forced her legs open and stuck two fingers inside her pussy, talking about how tight she was and how he was claiming her. She'd spent days being tortured and no one had cared enough to help.

Omar took notice of Monica lowering the gun and tried to attack her. "Stupid bitch! I'm gon' make you pay for pulling a gun out on me."

Snapped back into reality, tussling with Omar, Monica found that he was stronger than her, so it wasn't easy with his body weight on top of her. Monica begged, "No, please forgive me. I'll suck your dick, please just don't shoot me."

Omar contemplated on his next move. Stupidly, he figured why not get some head before he turned her over to Asad. He stood up and unzipped his pants, out of breath. "You better suck it good too, or you're good as dead."

Crawling over to Omar, Monica took his dick in her hands and stroked it up and down until it got hard. She put the head in her mouth and watched as Omar's eyes closed. With one quick movement, she pulled out the small machete she had tucked under her skirt and sliced off his dick.

Sling!

Omar hollered, "Aww, you fucking bitch!"

Even with his dick cut off, he was still talking shit as blood gushed all over the floor. Monica knew Too Short's performance would be over soon so she picked up her gun that was laying beside his body and shot.

BOOM! BOOM!

His body staggered to the couch, Omar crouched over with blood dripping from his mouth. His breath heaved in and out, trying to gasp for air. Thank goodness Too Short was performing and the music was blasting because nobody could hear the gun shots.

Monica dragged his body to the private bathroom in the dressing room stall and locked it. Then she cleaned up the blood and herself. Glancing in the mirror, she took a look at herself and broke down crying, not out of sympathy, but out of relief.

She sent the girls a text letting them know she would meet them at home and that she wasn't feeling well. Monica walked out of the hotel, pulled out her cell phone and called a taxi.

The party was coming to an end and Raine wasn't so sure about spending the night with Asad, but she was too close to turn back. Besides, she knew he wouldn't accept her excuses for too much longer. Asad had gotten a suite at the Marriot, he'd gone all out ordering up champagne and strawberries.

Raine looked around the room and she couldn't front, he did the damn thing. There was a Jacuzzi in the middle of the floor and candles traced the entire room.

"Relax, Raine. All I want to do is enjoy our night," Asad said.

Raine took off her shoes. "You went all out, this room is beautiful."

"This is just the beginning. You do right by me and I'll always treat you like a queen," Asad sat her down and begin messaging her feet.

"That feels too good. How are you single?" Raine asked.

"It's not easy to find a good woman who will stay by your side no matter what. There's a robe in the bathroom, go take a shower and let's hop in this water," Asad replied.

When she went into the bathroom, Raine removed her clothes and allowed the hot water to ease her mind. She thought about her and Asad possibly being together. Was it possible to be with a man that was such a monster to other woman? Her sisters in particular? Fuck no! He and all the bastards that had treated them like shit would pay.

Drying off, she put on her robe and went into the living room where she found Asad standing on the balcony.

"You cool?" Raine walked out to the balcony.

Asad turned towards her. Staring, he replied, "I'm straight, princess. Let me hop in this water so we can dip into the Jacuzzi."

Stepping into the Jacuzzi felt too good to Raine. She popped open the Moet and relaxed. Asad took so long that she almost dozed off, but once he walked out of the bathroom nude, she was wide awake.

Asad had the body of a God, not too big up top, but enough that his chest was purtruding and glistening from the water. His dick hung, slanging from side to side. Looking into her eyes, he saw her soaking him up. Looking up into his eyes, she cleared her throat, a little embarrassed that he'd caught her staring.

"See something you like?" Asad smirked.

"Maybe and maybe not," Raine mumbled.

Minutes went by and neither spoke. Running through Raine's mind was one thing, Remember he is a snake. Her pussy throbbing kept distracting her from focusing. It had become wet the moment Asad stepped out of the shower.

"Why you sittting over there? I don't bite, come here," Raine gestured with her finger.

Strolling over to Raine, he stepped between her thighs and spread her legs. He placed his hand on her breast and began to play with her nipples. Soft moans escaped her lips.

Asad picked her up and placed her on the side of the Jacuzzi. He blew on her pussy, Raine trembled in pleasure with her head held back. He kissed her from her feet to her thighs, looking up to see if she wanted him to stop. She was in a daze so Asad went in head first, placing his tounge to the opening of her pussy. He licked her slow from her ass to the her pussy lips.

Raine started moaning, "Damn, this shit feel too good." Asad continued to suck or her pearl tongue as his finger dipped in and out of her pussy.

Raine screamed, "Oh, shit, I'm about to cum! Don't stop, suck this shit!"

"Open your eyes," Asad demanded.

She did as she was told and looked him dead in the eyes. He looked up at her and continued eating her pussy.

"Oh shit, oh shit I'm cumming" Raine yelled.

In Asad's mind he was sure he wanted Raine and planned on getting her by any means necessary. He wasn't sure how she would take to him pimping out women and kids, though. Maybe he would just keep that part out until he knew how serious shit was.

One of the trap houses had been hit for a few keys and some stacks, while the team was partying it up. A page went to the team alarming them that the system had been tampered with. Rushing out of the party, no one spoke a word.

Jordan instructed the driver to drop them off at home. Rushing into the house, they changed, grab their straps and headed over to POP headquarters.

Nine deep in the Escalade, all that could be heard was straps being checked and bullets being loaded. Monica was still amped up from killing Omar so she'd had her Timbs laced up and her guns ready before everyone else made it home.

Moving as a unit into headquarters, Jordan shouted, "What the fuck happened?"

"It looks like they hit Oak Tree, not Stone Creek. Said some niggas from the West was asking who run the spot. They bounced and hours later Oak Tree was hit," Jack responded.

Snow barked, "Where were the lookouts?"

"Two got shot, they up at Mercy and the others went ghost," Jack confessed.

Alexis chimed in, "It was a set-up. How much you want to bet those that went ghost set us up?"

"Or got scared and bucked out," Christina interjected.

Jordan ordered, "Jack hold shit down, we're about to make a quick run."

Skirting off in the truck, the ladies had one thing on their minds. Blood. Jordan cruised down the street just to scope things out. The block was empty and only two dudes were out there standing. The truck they drove in must've stuck out because each man looked at the truck suspiciously. Jordan kept driving far enough away that they wouldn't notice them park and bounce out.

"Keep your straps close to you, any unsuspected movement, shoot. I want us all to come out of here breathing," Jordan instructed.

Snow cut in, "There were only two dudes out there, niggas done robbed our spot and have the balls to be out here grinding."

Seeing the ladies walk up, acting like they were looking to buy some blow, the men were hesitant, especially looking at their get up. But in Sac they were often surprised by who got high. Bird wondered why he should he give a fuck. As long as they had the cash to pay, he would supply.

Bird instructed Leo, "Go get these lovely ladies what they're asking for."

"You sure, boss. I don't want to leave you out here alone, no one is here to watch your back," Leo said, looking at the ladies skeptically.

"Nigga, I'm good, I got my piece right here. Besides, what can these bitches do for me besides get on their knees?" Bird chuckled.

"Aight," Leo ran off.

Hitting the corner to go get the blow, Bird stared at Alexis, eyeing her down. Alexis took that as him being interested and began to flirt "You are too cute, keep starring and I'm gon' have to take you home with me. How old are you?"

"Old enough."

Snow laughed, "I guess he told you."

"I thought y'all be deeper out here than this. You don't have no patnas to hook my sisters up with?" Alexis asked.

"Damn, are you here for blow or a date?" Bird asked.

Jordan replied, "Were here for you and your peoples."

Bird looked at Jordan like she had two heads. On impulse the girls drew out there straps and laughed at the reaction on Birds face.

"I'm gon' ask you this one time, where's the rest of your crew?" Alexis asked.

"What crew? It's just me and my homie out here slanging," Bird mumbled.

Guns cocked back. Snow placed her pistol to Birds head, "Nigga, you think we playing with you? I'm gone ask you this one time and lie to me if you want. Where is your peoples?"

Bird looked towards the building that Leo ran to. Alicia smirked. "That's more like it. Your services are no longer needed."

BOOM! BOOM!

There were two ways up to the trap house. Noise could be heard coming from the apartment like they were celebrating. Jordan thought it was best if they split up. While they were creeping up the stairs, Leo came rushing down to deliver the package of blow. Leo was a big dude, he stood five feet and weighed three hundred pounds. Christina put her finger to her lips, telling the girls to be quiet. Leo slowed down and took the last step. He must've sensed something wasn't right because he stopped and looked around.

Just as he was about to react, Christina muttered, "Yo, come here cutie." Leo knew something wasn't right and tried to run, but his fat ass wasn't fast enough. Before he could hit the corner, Christina was on his ass.

POW! POW!

His body hit the ground, making a loud ass thumping sound as it dropped.

"Help me drag his fat ass up under these stairs," Christina ushered Monica.

Music was blasting, no voices could be heard. Alexis thought it was a bad idea because they didn't know what they were up against. Jordan had a bad feeling as well. She pointed to Christina and Monica and gave them the signal to head out.

Chapter 11

After Asad gave Raine three nuts back to back, Raine couldn't take it anymore. Asad got out of the Jacuzzi with a smirk on his face like he was the man. Little did he know that the night had just begun.

Raine lay there motionless, trying to compose herself. Getting out of the Jacuzzi, she walked out to the patio where Asad sat naked and she dropped to her knees. She trailed kisses up his chest, to his neck and then his ear. He let out a soft moan. Just because of her touch his dick was rock hard.

She stroked him with her hand as she kissed his body. Making small kisses on his dick, she took him in her mouth little by little as she continued stroking.

Asad had the type of dick that could instantly make a woman horny just by the sight of it. It was nine inches long, thick, and black. Raine's pussy became moist as she bobbed up and down on his manhood. Asad held his head back and enjoyed the feel of Raine's warm mouth on his prized posession.

"Damn, Zariya, you sucking the shit out this dick," Asad mumbled.

Raine looked up, "You like it, baby."

"Hell yeah! Aww, shit, I'm about to cum, Ma!" Asad yelled.

"Cum for me, baby" Raine whispered.

On command, Asad's body began to shiver as his dick exploded in Raine's mouth. And just like the pro she was, she slurped up all his juices. She kept sucking his dick until it came back to life. Then after pulling out a condom and sliding it down with her mouth, Raine mounted his dick slowly. It was too big to just jump on.

Going up and down so that her pussy could adjust, she was finally being able to take it all in. She gave Asad the ride of his life. He started moaning and smacking her ass. To stop himself from cumming, he stood up and turned her around, bending her down so that her hands were wrapped around her ankles. Asad dove in, nice and slow with full force, almost making Raine's legs collapse.

"Oh shit! Hit that shit, baby!" Raine yelled.

Grabbing her arms, he held them behind her back and began hitting it harder. By the fifth stroke Raine started to cum, "Oh, shit, I'm cumming!"

"Take this dick, Zariya," Asad began digging deeper into her pussy, hitting it from all angles.

Then he felt himself about to nut, but he wanted one more nut up out of her. Asad demanded, "Cum with daddy."

Letting one of her arms go, he continued to fuck the shit out of her while he stroked her pearl tongue. As his body began to quiver while he was cumming, Raine came at the same time. They collapsed on top of each other, completely out of breath.

Asad sang in her ear, "It was the greatest sex I've ever had." They both broke out in laughter.

"You're so dumb," Raine cracked up.

Asad took her hand and led her into the shower. The two didn't utter a word, just bathed one another and dried off. Laying in each other's arms, their minds were in two different places. Asad was thinking that Raine was the one and in Raine's mind all she could think about was killing his ass.

The next morning they woke up, ate breakfast, and went their separate ways promising to talk later that evening. When Raine made it home, she knew something wasn't right. Going into the living room, she saw that the girls were quiet, watching Vince and Tamar.

"What's up ladies?" Raine yelled.

"Hey," Jordan replied.

"Damn, well good morning to you all too. What got everybody in a bad mood?" Raine asked.

Monica looked up from the Tv and said, "One of the spots was hit last night."

"What the fuck? Then what are we doing in the house when we should be out merking muthafuckas?" Raine yelled.

"We know who did it, but not enough about their squad to run up in there without being hurt. We gon' do this how we know best," Alexis responded.

"How do you know who did it? And how is that?" Christina jumped in.

"One of the dudes from the West's car was spotted skirting off. And how? The Power of the Pie!" Snow smiled.

Jordan's phone went off, interrupting the girls' thoughts. It was Isaac, he had been blowing her up ever since the little stunt he'd tried to pull at the event. She was gon' reply sooner or later, but right now wasn't the time.

"Who was that?" Snow questioned.

"You sure is nosy. Girl, you know that's Isaac's ass trying to explain why he showed up with a thot at the party," Jordan said.

"Men are just dumb. What the fuck was he thinking?" Monica laughed.

"He wasn't, but back to business. There is a party at some spot in West Sac, so ladies put on your best gear. We have some men to entertain."

Arriving back in the Bay, Asad's first stop was Treasure Island. He had to make sure business was cool and his hoes were behaving. Driving over the Bay bridge, his mind drifted to the night before when him and Raine fucked.

There was something about her that he was falling for. It wasn't her looks. She came off so innocent and smart and she was a freak in the bed. What more could he ask for? Joshua was at the gate, switching up the routine of the guard's pulling up. Asad entered his code and parked.

"Somebody look like they had a good time," Joshua clowned.

Asad grinned. "If you only knew."

"That party last night was on point, Omar must've dipped out not to much after you because I didn't see him once the shit was over," Joshua sang.

"Let me go check on these hoes. Hit up Omar and make sure he straight," Joshua barked.

Going into the first boarder house where the younger hoes were, Asad looked around and the place was a mess. His temper began to rise when he saw the women just lounging around like they were on vacation.

"What the fuck is this? Hoes on vacation around this muthafucka?" Asad shouted.

Women scattered and jumped to their feet, instantly cleaning up. None of the women wanted to make Asad angry because he was an animal when he was upset. He'd beat a woman half to death for not cleaning up a few dishes in the sink.

Asad sat on the couch, turned on some football and watched as the women cleaned. He wound up falling asleep and was awaken by Joshua screaming in his ear. Asad was still waking up and thought he'd heard wrong.

"You said what happened?" Asad asked.

Joshua shook his head. "Omar was found dead at the concert, somebody cut off his dick and shot his ass."

Asad froze for a minute, in shock about what Joshua had just told him. Someone was taking his team down. He had a feeling that whoever it was, was located in Sac. It wasn't a coincidence that two of his homies were killed in wack ass Sac.

"It has to be somebody from Sac and a bitch at that," Asad acknowledged.

"Why you say that?" Lavail, one of Asad's younger workers, asked.

"I just can't see no man cutting off the next nigga dick," Asad admitted.

Joshua thought back to the night at the party. "Maybe some nigga put his bitch up to it, I just can't see no hoe being able to catch Omar slipping."

"Let me bend a few corners and see if the streets are talking. Keep shit afloat and get ready for a war." Asad walked of out the door to his car.

Showing up at home in San Mateo, he went to his bedroom, took off his clothes and hopped in the shower. While the water relaxed him a bit, his mind drifted to the problem at hand. Asad knew he had to react and soon or the streets would think he was weak. But if it was a woman behind killing off his peoples, he was ready.

If there was one thing he knew how to do, it was handle a bitch. Going into the closet, he grabbed a duffle bag and filled it with clothes and stacks of money. It was time to take a trip to Sac and see what the word out there was. He also thought it would be a great opportunity to spend more time with Zariya.

Heading out to his QX56, he threw his bag in the back. Then he texted Joshua and a few of his other hitters, letting them know they were riding out to Sac for a few days.

Asad pulled off at the stop light off of Hesperian and texted Zariya.

Text: Hey, boo! I'm sliding back out there, hope to see you! Call you when I touch down.

Minutes went by and there was no reply. Maybe she was sleeping, he thought. Swooping up Joshua and a few others on the team, he headed down 80 towards Sacramento.

Blunts were being blazed and the Hennessey bottle passed around. There were a few newbies to the crew so Joshua had them come along so they wouldn't cause any problems at Treasure Island.

Asad decided it was best they stay somewhere in the cuts, where no one would think of looking for them. He copped a few rooms at the Courtyard Marriot off of Garden Highway. Heading to his room, he checked his cell phone, still no word from Raine. That now was making him suspicious.

Unpacking his bags, he tucked his money in the safe, strapped on his bullet proof vest and headed to the lobby. Ready to ride out to see what Sac life was like.

West Sac was a new area for the women. They never traveled too far out of North Sac, not because they were scared, there just wasn't any reason to. Some people in the crew wanted to take over all the spots in Sac, but that wasn't the plan. POP was about getting money and living by any means necessary.

The problem was the other drug spots in Sac weren't too happy that POP was taking over their clientele. The beauty of the POP crew was the fact that only so many knew who ran their crew. In all actually, it wasn't just one person, but a group full of sexy lethal woman.

Driving down Park Blvd, towards the club where the event was being held, Jordan pulled up across the street to observe the scenery. She noticed one of the dudes that had robbed the trap house. Sariya had done her homework on the crew on Facebook. Each was bragging about a lick they hit and posted pictures of them and the money they took. For POP, what they took was small, but enough to get someone killed.

Jordan uttered, "Snow, do what you do best and get us in the door without being patted down."

On que, Snow opened the truck door and strolled across the street looking like a runway model. She was sporting a mustard green short Bebe dress with some yellow Prada heels and just enough accessories to set it off. She wore nude makeup and her hair was up high in a bun with a few curls falling to the front.

"Damn, baby, you fine as a muthafucka! You got to save me a dance," the security guard hollered.

Snow looked up, giving him her best pose "Why, of course. That is if me and my girls can walk through without standing in this line?"

The security guard looked to where she was pointing and then down at her ass, "Hell yeah, come right in."

Woman and men were rambling on about how it was unfair that she cut the line as the woman got out of the Escalade ten deep, looking like Victoria Secret models. The men that were complaining shut their mouths and whistle instead, asking if they could come with them. Jack felt like the man being the only nigga with some boss bitches.

Jordan looked at the line going around the corner and snickered inside as she thought to herself, You got to pay the cost to be the boss. Snow stood on her tippy toes, leaned in and gave the security guard a kiss on the cheek before going inside.

After going through the double doors, the ladies saw that the club was moving. The D.J. was dropping hit after hit. Not feeling the standing up and walking around thing, Raine went to the bar to see if there were any more VIP booths available. There was one left, the biggest one.

The waitress said the price was nine hundred, like that would be a problem to pay. Raine whipped out her black card and told her to keep the bottles coming. The waitress' whole demeanor changed when she saw Raine whip out that black card.

All the girls were kidnapped at a young age. The moment they escaped Treasure Island and got established financially, each met with a financial advisor that helped them to build their portfolio and their credit.

To Jordan's surprise, Isaac was performing. She was happy to see him, but wouldn't let him know that. Isaac was the last thing she needed to be focused on. Seeing the dude that robbed them so close made her blood boil. Isaac's hype man was on stage freestyling, he went by the name of J fresh. He was on stage tearing shit up. Sac showed him much love, the thots saw money and was on his ass.

Isaac came on stage looking like a million bucks with a plain black t-shirt, black True's and the black/white 11's. His diamond chain was hangin' low, designed like a microphone with black and red diamonds. The chick he showed up with at the event was front and center, cherishing the moment of being his eye candy. If only the hoe knew that opportunity would soon be over once Jordan was back in the picture.

"Damn, bitch. Take a picture, it will last you longer," Christina joked.

Jordan cracked up, "Shut up, hoe!"

Men were coming up to the VIP all night trying to get at the women, but their mark had yet to notice them. That is until a few of the girls got up to head to the bathroom. That meant they had to pass Snap's table.

Snap was the head of the crew from the West, he was a short, chubby, dark skinned dude with braids going to the back. Cracking jokes with his homie, still on a high from the robbery, he looked up and locked eyes with Snow.

"Hey there, cutie. yYou should let me feel on that bootie!" Snap joked.

Snow wanted to smack the smirk off of his face, but she held her composure and smiled. "Is that how you approach a woman?"

Snap felt embarrassed because his crew starting laughing at his lack of response. So he replied, "My bad, ma. You should come enjoy the rest of the evening with me and my crew."

While trying to talk Snow into hanging with him, the other fellas fell in line and hollered at the other women. In all of the women's head, they thought, Check mate.

For the rest of the night, they hung out and pretended to be impressed by the money they were splurging on bottle service. Kris was trying to convince Jordan to go home with him. Of course she objected and he was pissed, but eventually he respected her decision. Isaac walked up with his thot on his arm, looking like he was ready to kill somebody.

Jordan smirked, "Hey, Isaac. And what's your name again, Cognac?"

"The name is Jasmine!" Jasmine snapped.

"My bad, Jasmine. This is Kris, Kris this is my friend Isaac," Jordan introduced the two.

"I'll see you around, friend," Isaac barked.

By the end of the night, everyone was loaded, ending up at Denny's. The fellas didn't want the night to end so Snap invited them over to his house to play bones. And just like that, the opportunity to kill their crew presented itself.

Chapter 12

On the radio, Asad heard about an event happening in West Sac on the drive up there. But by the time they made it, the club was letting out. He spotted Raine walking out the club with one of her girls. Just as they were getting in the carm Asad pulled up alongside of her.

"I guess you're avoiding me?" Asad asked with a slight attitude.

Raine hearing a familiar voice turned around in shock. "Hey, boo! What's up?"

"You tell me. I've been hitting your line since earlier and look, no reply," Asad explained, holding up his phone.

Sariya, Monica and Christina all dipped behind the tinted windows in the truck, trying not to reveal their identity.

"First off, Asad, a hello would be nice. Second, as you can see, I was out and I don't have my phone on me. Does it look like I have anywhere to carry a purse on this dress?" Raine twirled around, revealing her outfit.

Taking her all in, his dick jumped just by him glancing at her ass and thick ass legs. The crew took a glimpse as well. Raine had taken notice of the young girls with him and his new muscle.

"What you about to get into?" Asad asked.

Raine hopped into the truck and rolled down her window. "Shit, just chilling with my girls, having a ladies night. Hit my line once you get out of your feelings." Taping Monica on the shoulder so she could pull off, she was annoyed that they were way behind following Jordan and the dudes to Denny's.

Asad was pissed that she just sped off like that. He wanted to spend some time with her, but kissing her ass wasn't happening. Going back to the North, they strolled for hours checking out Sac scenery. Nothing stuck out until they exited W. El Camino and came across some apartments, the knocks was moving.

Pulling over to the side to check out the set up, he was impressed. The whole operation was smooth. One took the money, directed the knock to the other side of the street while the other one delivered his package while lookouts were on top of each building, tucked.

The spot was rolling and bringing in dough. Was it the product or just the location? Asad wondered. Instructing one of the young girls to go get a package, she hurried off and came back with a dime piece. Joshua kept complaining about how he was hungry so they stopped at Jack In the Box first then made their way back to the hotel.

Taking the package from Tameika, Asad broke it down once they were safely in the room. Then he smelled it and rubbed it on his gums. Instantly his mouth went numb. Chi-ching, he thought. Whoever was running the spot in Natomas was eating.

After everyone was full from eating at Denny's, they followed Snap to his home so they could play some bones and hang out a bit longer. He lived way out in Elk Grove. The neighborhood was quiet and security was patrolling. Offing them here and now wasn't gon' happen without someone getting locked up.

For the night, they just chilled and got to know one another. Of course the ladies' stories were all a bunch of lies. The men, however, told everything. I guess the saying was true, loose lips sink ships."

"It was fun kickin' it with you fellas, but it's time for us to turn it in," Jordan suggested.

Kris replied, "You don't want to spend the night?"

"Maybe one day, but for now my bed is calling my name. Ladies, let's bounce," Jordan advised.

As they walked outside they saw that the sun was coming up, they hadn't planned on being there so long. While in the car on the way home, Raine had told them how Asad popped up and almost spotted the others. Snow assured her that he wouldn't know who they were since they had changed their appearances and since it had been so long. Alexis wasn't so sure about that and couldn't help but wonder why Asad was back in Sac so soon.

"Raine, what's he here for? I though he left," Alexis questioned, the whole car went silent.

Raine thought about the question and shrugged her shoulders. "Honestly, I'm not sure. From my understanding he went back to the town after we kicked it."

"You need to find out." Christina demanded. "If he knows what were up to it could mean our life or our freedom."

After hearing those words, everyone was stuck in their of train of thought, just thinking about going back to Treasure Island had them shaken up.

When Raine made it home, the first thing she did was text Asad, inviting him to breakfast if he still was in town. Rather than wait for his response since it was still early, she took a quick shower and laid it down.

Just as she fell asleep, she got a text that read: I'm still here, will be in town for a few days on business. Let's meet up for breakfast at my hotel off Garden Highway.

Raine replied: Sure, see you in a few hours.

After setting her alarm for ten a.m., she then dozed off.

Waking up to the sound of her alarm, she was beyond exhausted. Raine willed herself from the bed and hopped in the shower, hoping the hot water would awaken her a bit. She felt a little refreshed when she exited the shower so she threw on some Hudson jeans, a sweater and a pair of pink Uggs.

As she Cranked up her charger, the engine roared. It was her new toy and she was in love with the power up under the hood. So many times men would pull alongside her, attempting to race her and she would leave their asses far behind.

Approaching the Courtyard Marriot where Asad was staying, she parked in front of the hotel's restaurant and checked herself in the mirror before going in. Marching through the lobby, Raine looked around before spotting him in the back sipping on coffee.

"Hey there, handsome!" Raine strolled over and gave him a hug and a kiss on the cheek.

Asad blushed. "Aren't you a sight for sore eyes this morning. You looking like you haven't slept at all."

"No, I didn't get much sleep last night. Partied with the girls and then we went to an after gathering once the club let out."

"I thought you would've spent the night with me." Asad expressed.

A waiter walked up just as Raine was about to reply. While the waiter was taking their order Raine took that as an opening to calm herself down. "I will take a mimosa, a Denver omelet, some oatmeal, and a cup of coffee please."

Raine cleared her throat with finality when the waiter walked off. "First off, I don't remember being invited. Then you pull up and embarrass the shit out of me, talking about some text message bs. And finally, I thought you were going back to Oakland when you left me the other morning."

He looked away, not wanting her to see that he was hooked and wanted to spend as much time as possible with her in his arms.

Gazing into her furious face, he manned up and admitted, "I was wrong. I assumed that when you saw me you would invite yourself. And I did go home, but some shit popped off with my business. I'm here to get to the bottom of things."

"Shit like what?" Raine grilled.

Asad answered, "One of my boys was killed the other night at the party. This is the second time someone has offed one of my peoples here in Sac. I'm here to get to the bottom of it, as a matter of fact, maybe you can help me?"

"Help you how?" Raine urged.

"You live here, last night I was going to the hotel and noticed that somebody is out here eating. Off of W. El Camino. Whoever dude is has a great operation, perhaps he knows something," Asad made clear.

Raine sat there as if she was considering helping. "All I know is that whoever it is that's running it over there isn't to be fucked with. I heard in the street that he had killed some dude for just coming around asking questions. I mean what kind of business are you in that people are knocking off your friends?"

"I hustle. I'm not small time so there are people out there looking to take over my empire."

"How long are you in town for?" Raine asked.

"Just for a few days."

After eating breakfast they retreated back to Asad's room. Hours of sexing each other later, they dose off watching Tamar and Vince.

119

Each girl was still knocked out when Raine made it back home. She went into each of their rooms, calling an emergency meeting. Everything she and Asad talked about was weighing heavy on her brain.

Changing into something more comfortable, Raine went into the kitchen and cooked breakfast. One by one the women came down for the meeting. By looking at Raine, they could sense it was something serious.

"Okay, were up. Now what's the reason for the emergency meeting?" Alexis asked.

Raine sat down and took a deep breath. "I went to see Asad this morning and he is looking for whoever killed his two patnas here in Sac."

"What do you mean two of his boys were killed here? We only murked one!" Jordan hollered.

Monica raised her hand. "Actually there was two. At the event, Omar had spotted me and followed me to the back where the dressing rooms were, rambling on about how he was gone tell Asad and take me back to Treasure Island."

"What the fuck! Why didn't you tell us?" Jordan yelled.

"We been running nonstop, trying to off the niggas in the West. It wasn't like I wasn't going to tell you all," Monica stated, looking around the room.

No one said anything. Different emotions were running through each of their minds. And each lady came to the same conclusion, either it was Asad or them. They knew that eventually they would kill him, but not so soon. They needed more time because Jordan wanted to make him and his team crumble individually.

During the meeting, Raine let them know where Asad and his team were staying. Tonight they would be executing his new lieutenant and whoever else was with him.

"Our plan can still work. Raine, you continue doing what you do. He will soon need you when he learns his men are falling," Alexis advised.

"What makes you so sure?" Raine questioned.

Alexis squinted her eyes, trying to read Raine's thoughts. "I know men. Asad is a bitch, he is going to go into hiding and since he can't be without you, you will be the first he will call to take with him."

Jordan stood up at the head of the table, "It's as simple as this, take him out or be taken out!" Raising her glass to make sure everyone was on board, she was happy to see that of course they all chose to knock Asad down.

The mission to take out Asad's lieutenant didn't call for all the women to be present, there was a lot on the girls' plate. Asad was getting close and they had to take care of the dudes from the West before word got out on the street about them not retaliating. If one crew could get away with hitting the spot others would b soon to follow.

Christina, Red, Monica, Alicia, and Sariya went to chill with Snap at the pool hall. Those women had dealt with nothing but the harsh side of life. One would think, by looking from the outside in, that they had it all. If people only knew what those woman had been through.

Being free meant a lot, but they still felt trapped and afraid as long as Asad was on the loose. For a child to be stripped of their innocence, molested, beaten, and starved for weeks, that showed just how depraved Asad really was. All of them were obligated to Snow, Jordan, and Alexis for taking them as well when they escaped. Sacramento was a little cold, but the sun still shined.

Jordan went into the kitchen and began preparing all of their favorite foods. Before the night's events, they needed some family time. She went to the grocery store and gathered all the ingredients needed for garlic crab, shrimp and scallop fettuccini Alfredo, fresh salad, and garlic bread. And Snow made her famous banana pudding.

An hour and a half later, the eight of them gathered around the table and grubbed. Afterwards, they parked in front of the television and caught up on the reality shows.

Watching Love and Hip Hop, cracking up at that broad Diamond, they joked about how she had to be the dumbest on chick tv. Hoe was dating a dude for two years, didn't know his address, and to make matters worse he only gave her the dick in the car. That hoe thought she was doing something when she popped up on his ass in New York Burt she felt stupid when he placed her at his friend's house instead of in the house with him.

"This hoe is too dumb. What mother denies her kid, though?" Sariya laughed.

Jordan burst out, "The hoe is a comedian, there's no way I would've taken a man serious who only gives me the business in the car."

"No, what took the cake is when he took Diamond to his friend's house and not his. Talking about he has trust issues. Nigga, please!" Alexis said.

By seven 'o clock the women all went in opposite directions. Before they headed out, Sariya suggested a prayer.

"Dear, Father God, we come to you and ask you to forgive us and be with us all tonight as we embark upon this journey. In Jesus' name we pray, Amen." Sariya prayed.

The first thing they did was meet up with Wayne to get a scrapper that couldn't be traced. When they were done with that, Snow pulled onto Garden Highway to the back of the hotel where Asad and his crew wer staying. Then they marched up to the front desk to check in under an alias. After that they were off to their room to change.

Down the hall, Asad was holding a meeting with his crew to see what ideas they had on figuring out who was behind knocking them down. Joshua recommended that they go to the functions and see who was who in Sac. He figured doing that might lead them to the right person.

A while later, after Raine had left, Asad got to thinking about what his next move should be. He wasn't gon' just stand still while someone was offing his team. Ending the meeting, each decided on going to a club in Old Sac. Joshua was leaving his room and bumped into Jordan, not knowing who she was, he tried to holla.

Giving him excuses on why she couldn't exchange numbers, Jordan walked over to the vending machine which happened to be across from Asad's room. Yes, it was risky being that close to him and she hoped that he didn't recognize her. Glancing up from the soda machine, she caught Joshua still starring at her before closing his door.

On her way back to the room, Jordan stopped and turned around, blocking the view of the camera. She disarmed the fire alarm, placing a timer on it so that by the time they killed Joshua it would give a distraction for them to be able to escape. Now that she knew where he was staying, it was just going to be a matter of getting in his room unnoticed and killing him without alerting anyone else staying at the hotel.

Back in the room, Snow and Alexis were strapping up and putting on their body armor to protect them from being killed. When Jordan made it back to the room with the location of Asad's new muscle, the women were ecstatic at the idea of it being so easy. The plan was to be in and out before being noticed.

Standing in a circle, praying for their plan to work out, they walked out of the room with one thing on their minds. Kill or be killed. Strolling down the hall in her all black cat suit, Snow saw a maid enter the maids break room.

When she walked in as if she belonged and the maid tried to object to her being in there, Snow pulled out her chrome .45, held it up to the woman and politely demanded, "The key to room four-oh-seven, please?"

Reaching into her apron, the lady handed the keys over and took a breath of relief once Snow put her gun down. To her surprise, Snow didn't kill her, just knocked her over the head with the butt of her gun. Then she tied her up so she couldn't fuck up their plans.

"This bitch is on her shit," Jordan whispered and smiled.

Alexis knocked on Joshua's door and uttered, "Room service, room service." Leaning her ear to the door to see if there was any sounds coming from inside, she heard nothing. Alexis looked to the girls and gave them a thumbs down, letting them know that no sounds could be heard.

Just as Snow was about to put the key card in to open the door, a shot was let off.

BOOM!

"You muthafucka's gon' have to come harder them this," Joshua shouted.

Knowing Joshua's gun was heard, Jordan knew they had to move quickly, She shot the lock off of the door and went in shooting. Alexis and Snow followed suit. All you could hear for miles away was the sound of canons going off.

BOOM! BOOM!

With a bullet catching him in the shoulder, he fell to the floor still shooting his peace and hitting snow in the leg.

Snow screamed in pain, "Oh shit, he shot me!"

Jordan looked down at her sister, blood started running, gushing out and Jordan became furious. Alexis pulled Snow up as Joshua was still shooting with one arm gushing out blood. He continued letting off some rounds but he made the mistake of focusing on only Alexis and Snow and forgetting there was a third person in the room.

Jordan crawled from behind the bed. POW! POW! TAT! TAT! Shooting Joshua in his chest, she smiled when the impact from the .45 landed him on his back, holding his chest.

Jordan quickly rushed over to him before he could pick his pistol back up. Then she let off a final shot to the head, killing Joshua instantly. While Alexis held one of Snow's arms, Jordan grabbed the other and together they charged to their room. As soon as their door closed, others could be heard opening. That's when the fire alarm went off.

That alarm gave all hotel occupants five minutes to evacuate. After quickly changing their clothes, Alexis wrapped up Snow's leg and they rushed out of the hotel room as if it was really on fire. Alexis could hear Asad in the distance yelling, "What the fuck!"

In her head she knew he'd found his right hand man and she couldn't hold in the smile. The joy she felt for the revenge they were getting on Asad was like a breath of fresh air.

Chapter 13

Ace's Bar and Pool Hall was cranking. It was the main location for Sacramento residences if they wanted a good drink and to mingle. Christina was pissed that they had to hang with Snap and his crew, especially with all of the hot men strolling around the bar. Alicia went over to the bar and ordered a bottle of Hennessey along with some tequila for the girls, she was ready for the shit to go down so she could get back to Jack.

Things between the two had become serious, they were now dating exclusively. Jack was parked outside of the pool hall, chilling with some of the fellas from the crew. Alicia's ear piece looked like a blue tooth so everything could be heard on his end.

Jack was beginning to get pissed at that nigga Snap for trying to get into Alicia's panties. Lamont was cracking jokes about how Snap was trying to dig into his woman. Taking a sip of the Patron, he laughed and said "Fuck y'all! That nigga's about to meet his maker in all due time."

Snap whispered in Alicia's ear, "We can go to my house and I'll eat that kitty all night long."

Laughing, she replied, "Is that right, daddy? You think you can handle this pie?"

"Hell yeah!" Snap was excited of the thought of getting between Alicia's thighs. He really wanted her homegirl, Jordan, but she would do.

"Damn, daddy, you got this pussy wet just by talking about eating her. Fuck going way to your house, we can get a room at Motel 6," Alicia cooed.

Not giving her a chance to change her mind, Snap told the crew it was time to bounce. Jack cranked up the car and headed to Motel 6 off of Richards. Minutes later, he could hear them all piling up in the car on their way. Lamont hopped out the car and strolled to the front desk to get a room and to reserve one for Alicia so they could be in the room adjoined to them.

Finally pulling off the exit, Sariya stopped at the liquor store across the street from the motel to get some more alcohol. Or so the men thought. Monica went inside with her and purchased some anti-freeze. Then she dipped off into the bathroom to pour the anti-freeze in the mountain dew bottles. The drinks from the bar had them tipsy, but not enough that they would be off their toes.

"Can't believe y'all still trying to drink," Kris said.

Chrsitina replied, "Heck yeah! Turn down for what?"

Alicia went into the motel to pay for the room, the lady at the front desk handed her the key to the room Lamont had reserved.

Leaving the girls, Christina acted as if she was going to the vending machine for some ice, looking back to make sure she wasn't being followed the entire time.

On the way back from the ice machine, she stopped at the room Jack and the crew was hanging out in. Knowing she couldn't be gone for too long, she took off her shirt and strapped up with a bulletproof vest. Then she tucked one .38 under her skirt and another one in her purse.

When Christina made it back to the girls, the music was blasting and Sariya was at the sink mixing up the drinks. Walking over, Christina handed Sariya the ice, then turned around to look at Alicia.

"I think I had too much to drink." Alicia rose to her feet and rushed off to the bathroom.

Christina went in after her, saying as loud as she could, "Sis, you alright?" Then she closed the door behind her.

Snap knocked on the door, "You okay, baby girl?"

"I'm cool, just too much Patron. I'll be out in a minute," Alicia assured him.

Going into her purse, Christina handed Alicia a strap, then walked back into the room. Each person had a glass in their hand and Sariya walked around making sure the men's drinks stayed filled to the rim.

Marcus started to become impatient, he was ready to jump deep into Sariya's pussy. Pulling her to him forcefully, he tongue kissed her. The kiss made her think of all the times at Treasure Island that she had been raped. Thinking about her past, she bit down on his tongue.

Marcus jumped up and yelled, "Bitch, what the fuck you bite me for?"

Sariya smiled, "I thought you liked it rough, daddy."

Marcus charged towards her, ready to smack the smile off of her face, but he was pulled back by Snap and Kris. Snap knew Marcus had a bad temper and word around the hood was that he had a habit of beating up women.

Marcus calmed down and went out to get some air. For a second, Sariya started to panic. She went to follow him to apologize, but as she walked outside she saw Cliff already talking to him and smoking on a cigarette. Cliff looked her way and gave her a nod to go back to the room.

Opening the bathroom door, Alicia yelled, "We in the building!" That was the que to Jack to get ready to come in with the guns blazing. The anti-freeze started to kick in and Kris' eyes were doing a dance as they started to roll to the back of his head.

"Snap, you looked fucked up, boo. You cool?" Alicia played concerned.

Snap opened his eyes and replied, "I'm fucked up Ma, come here."

Wandering over to where Snap was sitting, Alicia sat on his lap and whispered in his ear, "Now you didn't think you would take my shit and live did you?"

Shoving Alicia off his lap, he barked, "Bitch, what you just say?" Trying to stand to his feet, Snap staggered back and fell. The effects of the anti-freeze had him dizzy. Just when he tried to get up again, he was looking up at the barrel of Alicia's gun. Kris heard the commotion of his homie and tried to see what was going on, but Christina stopped him dead in his tracks with her .38 pointed at his chest.

"You need to sit that ass back down. You won't be going nowhere no time soon," Christina insisted.

Kris held his hands up, ready to piss on himself. "What's this about? Take what the fuck you want, hoe, and bounce."

Christina looked over to Alicia and started cracking up. "Your broke ass don't have shit I want. You niggas are too dumb, thought you could hit our spot and live?"

With his eyes half shut, Snap muttered, "What the fuck are you talking about?"

"The spot you and your homies hit in Natomas, that's me and my family shit you took," Alicia explained.

Kris' eyes opened up as big as saucers. In shock of who those hoes were, he started to think of a way out. But Sariya walked in with four niggas and he knew then that his life was over. Immediately, he made up his mind. If he was going to die, he was going to do it like the boss nigga he was.

Jack walked in and went over to Snap, hitting him with the butt of his gun. "Nigga, that's for trying to fuck my broad."

Standing off to the side, letting Jack handle those niggas his way, Lamont didn't say anything. He was the one in the crew that knew how to keep his cool, but if you got on his bad side there wasn't a way out.

Jack and Cliff were going back and forth, asking those niggas who was the link in our crew. After thirty minutes of beating them close to death, and still neither one said a word, Lamont had had enough.

He strolled over to Snap. "You know what, dude, if you just give us one person, I'll let you walk."

"Nigga, fuck you!" Snap shouted.

At that point, Lamont lost his patience. Then grabbed Snap's hand, took out the pliers, and cut off one of his fingers. Blood gushed out as Snap grabbed ahold of whatever piece of his finger was left on his hand and then he passed out from the pain. But he was awakened by the water that Alicia threw on his face.

"I'm gon' ask you one more time, homie, wake up and stop passing out like a little bitch," Lamont ordered.

Getting tired of him crying and bitching about his finger, Sariya walked over to him and shot him twice in the chest.

BOOM! BOOM!

She said, "He wasn't giving any information."

Kris suddenly rose to his feet, charging at Jack. But he was no challenge for Jack because Jack was five-nine and all muscle. Jack slammed his fist to Kris' back as Kris held tight to his waist.

Then, releasing his hold and looking up, he pleaded for his life. "Man just let me go. All I know it's some nigga from the South, but he grind in Natomas. He is closer than what you think." Before he could reveal a name, Cliff walked over to him and blew his brains out.

BOOM! BOOM!

Lamont rushed Cliff. "What you do that for?"

"Cause nigga, he wasn't gon' tell us shit and we're wasting time," Cliff replied.

"Nigga, you don't know that. Let me find out it was you!" Lamont barked.

Cliff looked away, "Nigga, you got me fucked up."

For a second Cliff thought his identity was going to be revealed. He had to kill Kris before the dude gave him up and his own life was over.

Snow went into panic mode once making it back to their room, she was losing a lot of blood. Alexis helped her out of her pants, wrapped up the womb and out the door they went. The pain of the gunshot made her go into shock and staring at her reflection in the mirror didn't make it any better.

Jordan went ahead of the two to reach the car. Opening up the exit door of the hotel, she could hear the police and fire trucks getting close. Making it to the car, she threw the bag of guns in the trunk and pulled right in front of the exit door.

"Come on, we have to bounce!" Jordan urged.

Once they were safely in the car, Jordan pulled towards the back streets going in the opposite direction of the police. She was headed towards Truxel and onto W. El Camino. Reaching under the seat, Alexis sent a text to the doctor they'd added to the payroll after Christina had been shot. The doc said he would meet them at his office off of Northgate in ten minutes.

Arriving at the doctor's location, both girls hopped out to help Snow inside. She was doing her best to keep from falling asleep.

"Is she going to be okay?" Alexis hollered.

Dr. Lee instructed, "Lay her down. She has lost a lot of blood, I can't say for certain, but she needs to go into surgery. I need to remove the bullet and I'm hoping it's not too close to any organs." He went into the drawer and pulled out a needle. Then he gave her a shot to stop her wound from getting an infection.

Next, he hooked her up to an IV and filled it with fluids to help her with the dehydration and pain. Going to his office, he called for help to assist him while operating. Snow wasn't fully aware of her surroundings because she kept blacking out. The medicine Dr. Lee gave her helped a little with the pain, but she was losing so much blood.

Once the woman arrived, Dr. Lee introduced his assistant. "This is Margaret, she will be helping me with the surgery. I will need you two to step out."

Walking out of the door as the doctor had instructed, Jordan embraced Alexis and the two broke down crying in each other arms.

Taking a deep breath, Alexis advised, "Sis, go get shit together we're still riding dirty. I will hit you when I know something."

Hugging each other before saying goodnight, Jordan made her way to one of the drop off spots where they got rid of evidence. She parked at the gate off Richards. Walking through Discovery Park and using the flashlight to guide her, she looked around to make sure no one was watching. Then she dumped the pistols in the river.

Standing there until they floated to the bottom and thinking of the nights festivities had her on overdrive with her emotions. Tonight she could've lost her sister. Wiping the tears away, Jordan tossed the duffle bag into the trash and set it on fire. As it went into flames, she said a silent prayer and made her way back to the car. Back on the freeway, she realized they forgot to dump the car. She then sent a text to Wayne letting him know she was on her way.

Driving down 80, she took the long way so she wouldn't have to go back to where the scene was. Jordan thought about Isaac and their last evening together. The one thing that man knew how to do was make her feel like she was all that mattered. Nevertheless, the moment he learned she wasn't ready for a commitment, he went running to the next woman and that's what hurt. She'd been thinking that what they shared was more than a nut, at least that's what she was hoping.

Taking the Watt exit, she drove down and made a turn onto Arden Way. While waiting on Wayne, Jordan called Isaac and was not surprised that a woman answered the phone.

"Can I speak to Isaac?"

Jasmine looked at the caller ID. "Jordan, I would appreciate it if you wouldn't call my home."

"Sweetie, that isn't your home. You're just there filling my spot while I am handling business. Truthfuly, if I wanted you gone tonight, he would serve you your walking papers!" Jordan laughed.

Jasmine became furious at the thought and replied, "That's what the fuck he is not about to do!"

"Ha, ha! You don't know about the power of the pie?" Jordan asked.

"The what?" Jasmine was lost.

Jordan shook her head, "Is he there? I will prove it."

"Yep!"

"I'll be there in a minute, please have your shit out of my house by the time I get there." Jordan demanded before she hung up.

Jasmine was pissed to think that bitch was about to come there and throw her out. She had to be out of her rabid ass mind. Isaac loved her and wouldn't dare put her out.

Pulling off the lot in her 2013, 750 BMW, Jordan drove towards Rancho Cordova and exited towards Isaac house. He lived in a secluded area. Punching in her code, she was surprised to find that it was still the same. It was their anniversary.

Parking in front of the garage, she looked in the mirror and applied some clear Mac gloss. Taking a deep breath, she stepped out of the car and went to his door, not wanting to just walk in even though she could have.

She rang the doorbell and sang, "Honey I'm home."

Jasmine opened the door barefoot, wearing black leggings and with her hair pulled into scarf. Jordan had to admit that even dressed down, Jasmine was cute for a simple bitch. But cute or not, the hoe had to go.

Jasmine was shocked that the bitch really came. Isaac was in the game room entertaining some of his friends so he hadn't heard the door. "Bitch, you must be crazy coming to my house." She jabbed her finger in Jordan's face.

Jordan laughed and walked past her, shoving her out of the way so hard that she fell to the floor. To her surprise, Jasmine got up and hurried behind her. Hearing where the racket was coming from, Jordan barged in on the fellas and stood in front of the television.

"Honey, I'm home. Hey Gene, Howard."

Isaac stared in shock that Jordan was there. Then he reacted. "What are you doing here?"

"Is that the way you great your wife. I'm home, baby. I see we have company so I'm going to go make a run and before I get back, fire the help," Jordan smirked, looking over where Jasmine stood.

"The help? Bitch you got me fucked up. Isaac, you gon' just let her come in our home and disrespect me like that? You better get this bitch before I do!" Jasmine said, getting ready to charge at Jordan. That was until Isaac pulled her back.

Shrugging his shoulders and releasing her arm, "My bad, Jasmine," he told her. "But you heard her, you have to bounce. Wifey's home"

"What?" Jasmine asked in disbelief. Not long ago he had her bent over the bathroom sink giving it to her and now he was throwing her out. No, they hadn't made it official, but it was falling into place in all due time.

Jordan looked Jasmine in the face and leaned in. "Some advice woman to woman, before you crawl into the next woman's spot, ensure that the spot is actually available. I could've told you we weren't over if you would have just asked. Babe, can you please change the locks when she leaves?"

"Bitch, you got me fucked up!" Jasmine then got ahold of Jordan.

With Jasmine throwing wild punches, she caught Jordan once in the chest. Taking a step back, Jordan hit Jasmine in the face, throwing her off balance. Then she grabbed Jasmine by the hair, flipped her on the ground and stomped her out.

Straddling her, Jordan continuing to go in on her face. She had so much built up anger in her that it all came out on Jasmine. Jasmine had thought for sure that she had Jordan by her body size, but she was overwhelmed by the damage her face had just received.

Isaac finally pulled Jordan off of Jasmine and then helped Jasmine up. Inspecting her and seeing that she was okay, Isaac put his attention back on Jordan.

"This hoe came at me, she should've known better. Have her shit gone when I come back. Howard, Gene, I owe you a night out for ruining your night," Jordan laughed and then went to her car.

How badly she wished Isaac had been home alone. She needed a shoulder to lean on to just let it all out. Her fear was that Isaac wouldn't fuck with her if he knew her background and the things she had to endure to survive. That's why she pulled away. That's why she dismissed him when he gave her that ultimatum.

Chapter 14

On the drive back to the spot, Jack got to thinking about what went down at the motel and something didn't sit right with him. For sure there was a snitch in the crew. He thought he knew who it was and it pissed him off. Because he was the one that had brought dude into the set, it would be his job to take him out.

Jack dropped Cliff off to his ride while him and Lamont rode to the spot to check on things. The girls were loaded and still amped from the night's events. Jack dropped them off as well since it was late, and not much was moving. Then Jack and Lamont continued cruising both with their minds heavy.

Lamont pulled out a blunt wrap, broke down the weed and rolled up. Pulling on the blunt and passing it over to Jack, he barked "I don't trust your boy, something not right with him."

"Yeah, I feel it, I need to be sure though. Take him off the ya-yo and the money. Matter fact, let's change shit up. We can't let the girls know tonight. Knowing them, they gone want him murked tonight." Jack advised.

Handing Lamont the blunt back, he sent a text to Jordan.

Jack: We need to meet up ASAP, sis!

Jordan: Slide through to the house, be there in 10.

Opening up the garage door, Jordan pulled her car in and walked into the house. Everyone was in attendance that mattered minus Alexis and Snow. Before going into the living room to join the crew, Jordan went into her room and showered. Throwing on some sweats and a t-shirt, she made her way back downstairs, going straight to the bar to pour her a shot of Patron.

Turning around, Jordan asked, "How did it go tonight?"

"I think there's a snitch within our crew. I think I have an idea of who it is," Jack replied.

Jordan sat down next to Lamont. "Let me guess, Cliff."

"How did you know?" Lamont questioned.

Jordan looked at him like he had three eyes. "He is new to the crew so of course I had him followed to see if he can be trusted. And he is from the West but just perpetrated like he was from the South. Bruh, you know what you have to do right?"

"Taking that snitch nigga out," Jack barked.

"There's one more problem, though. I left Marcus with him and if he is a snitch that mean Marcus is still breathing."

Taking the top off the bottle of Patron and guzzling it down, Jordan spoke. "Bruh, fire up the blunt. If it's not one thing, it's another. Snow has been shot, she had to go into surgery and now we have Marcus and this lunatic Cliff on the loose. Lamont put a price tag on both their heads and I have to tuck Snow away until this beef ends."

"OMG! Why you didn't tell us this first? How is she?" Sariya shouted.

Jordan looked at her like she had lost her mind. "Not sure yet. I had to move fast and dump the scrapper. Alexis said she would call once Snow was out of surgery."

"Well Cliff don't know that we know he is a rat. Let's use him to lead us to Marcus, that way we will kill two bitches at once," Jack recommended.

"That's why I love you, bruh! You and Lamont change up the whole set-up. Corn, you're on the ya-yo and Jack you on the money. Every day, switch it up," Jordan ordered.

Lamont muttered, "It's about time, sis. You and the others show your face to the streets, that's why nigga's are trying to move in."

Strolling over to the door to put on her shoes, Jordan stumbled and fell to the floor. For the first time she had shown weakness in front of the crew, not being able to compose herself any longer.

Lamont went over to her and helped her up. "Come on, sis, it's gon' be okay."

"Let's go check on Snow," Alicia offered.

Gathering into the car to check on Snow, Raine got a text message from Asad.

Asad: Babe, I'm gon' see you in a bit, some shit went down, I'll holla.

142

She didn't even reply. Her sister was all that mattered at the moment.

There were no cars out, just the family and they were all in deep thought about how quickly life had gone from sugar to shit. Arriving at the doc's office, Jordan saw that Alexis was passed out in the waiting room. Sariya tapped her on the shoulder and she had woke up.

Alicia asked, "How is she?"

"She made it through the surgery. I was waiting on the doctor to move her into a room," Alexis said.

Making it into Snow's room, the only sound Alexis heard was that of the machines and the sobs from the others crying. Snow was one of the toughest in the crew. Jordan and Alexis knew her best, but not ever had they seen her so fragile. That had them bothered.

While Snow was in surgery, Alexis got to thinking about how she wouldn't mind settling shit with Asad and getting out of the game. Dr. Harley did as promise and had gotten a divorce. He and Alexis were seeing each other again. Nothing too serious, just dating to see where they would go. Alexis thought he would think less of her since he'd met her through an escort service.

The crew may have messed up by stepping into the drug game. Things were good for POP and money was flowing. Red was running the girls lately since the other part of their business kept them so occupied. After making a couple hundred thousand, money and living like celebrities became addicting.

Jordan whispered, "Shit is all bad. Cliff not cool, him and Marcus are on the loose. We have to watch our back until they're both taken out."

"I always said something wasn't right about dude," Alexis replied.

"Asad has been blowing me up. He went back to the Town and said he would hit me," Raine interjected.

Monica asked, "Where is Red?"

"She's with a client. He is a high roller, she has Black watching her," Sariya responded.

Jack walked over to Snow's bedside and rubbed her face. "She looks like an angel. We have to get her moved up out of here."

The moment Jordan was getting ready to speak up, the doctor walked in.

"Can we move her to another place until she heals?" Sariya questioned.

Dr. Lee pushed his glasses up. "Not tonight. Tomorrow I'll have her ready to be transported."

With that information, everyone left except Lamont and Alexis. They stayed to hold it down until the following day, not wanting to leave Snow alone and unarmed.

Being dropped off at Isaac's house, Jordan knocked on the door. A half-awake Isaac opened the door standing in only a pair of boxers. As she walked past him and into the house, he grabbed her from behind and led her to his bedroom.

Eyeing him with her pussy on fire, she sat on the bed and allowed him to stand over her a bit. Hugging him from the waist down, she slid her hand into his boxers and the boxers dropped to the floor.

Seeing how hard his dick was had her pie dripping and her mouth watering. Slowly, she guided his dick into her mouth. Isaac just tilted his head to the side watched Jordan go to work on his dick as small moans escaped his mouth. There was something about how that woman sucked his dick that no other woman could do.

Fully erect and not able to contain himself any longer, Isaac pushed Jordan back and took off her sweats only to be rewarded with the sexiest pussy he ever saw. It was nicely trimmed and smelled like vanilla.

Slowly, he trailed kisses up her thighs. Taking one of his fingers and inserting them into her pussy, he smiled when Jordan arched her back out of pure joy and let out moans. Isaac blew on her pussy, urging Jordan to put it in his face. She grab ahold of his head and guided him to the pie.

"Damn, daddy, I want to feel that big dick inside me," Jordan pleaded.

Opening her legs more, Isaac was on a mission to make her nut until she passed out. Slurping up her juices, he could tell she was close to her first orgasm. Her pearl tongue was swollen and her moans had picked up.

Then Jordan hollered, "Oh, shit! I'm cumming, oh, shit!! Ok, babe, I can't take it no more."

Standing to his knees to give Jordan a full view of his dick, he then laid between her legs. Jordan scooted back as she played with her pussy, teasing him. Isaac kissed her nipples while playing with her pussy with the tip of his dick.

Jordan begged, "Put him in, daddy."

Isaac grinned and guided all nine inches of his dick into her pie.

"Stop playing with her and give it to me," Jordan demanded.

Isaac barked, "Shut up and enjoy this dick."

An hour of fucking and making up finally had them tapped out. Jordan was unable to sleep so she went to the kitchen to get something to snack on and drink. Opening up the fridge, she pulled out a slice of cheese, butter, and some grapes. She made a grilled cheese sandwich and some peppermint tea.

Her heart fluttered when she looked at the refrigerator door and saw a picture of her, Alexis, and Charles on a double date at Boiling Crab in South Sac. Sitting on the stool eating her grilled cheese sandwich and allowing the peppermint sleepy time tea to relax her, she jumped when Isaac walked behind her and put his arms around her.

"Oh, shit! You scared the shit out of me," Jordan said, in shock.

Isaac smiled, going into the fridge to get a water. "It's just me, who else would it be?"

"I don't think you want me to answer that question."

"So what made you come back to me?" Isaac asked.

Jordan contemplated what to say and decided honesty was best. "I been through a lot in the last few days, shit the last few years. I was looking for peace and thought of the last place I felt at peace. I always somehow found peace when I was with you, you know? Hope to finally be happy."

"I'm always here for you, but I can't do the back and forth thing, J. Either you're here for good or you're not. I have a lot going on as well and to have a solid woman by my side would make things better for me."

"I need to tell you something, Isaac, but it can't leave this room. It may make you change your mind about wanting to be with me. I come from a rough background."

Isaac interrupted, "Well all have, J."

"You gon' let me finish. I was kidnapped when I was fourteen, taken to a place in San Francisco where this group of men pimped out little girls and women. I have been used and abused by so many men, it's not even funny. For months I and my sisters came up with a plan to escape and it worked. We got away and came here to Sac, things been going really good for us."

"Damn, I didn't know there are men out there so cold."

"Believe it. That's not it, though. I run one of the biggest escort service in the U.S."

"What the fuck!" Isaac yelled.

He looked at her for a moment, wondering if he had heard her correctly. When he was sure he had, he turned his back on her and walked away. Isaac had no idea how to handle what she'd said so he went into a room where he could be alone and think. He really wanted Jordan, but what she said was a lot for any man to take in.

Letting him go to absorb all that she had just told him, Jordan went into the bathroom and took a shower. Hopping out, she rubbed herself down with baby lotion, threw on one of Isaacs t-shirts, and crawled into bed. She hadn't told him all of it, she'd told him just enough to see just how he would weather the storm.

Later the next day, Cliff met up with Marcus at one of the under spots in West Sac. He was a bit shaken up after he was dropped off by Jack. He knew for sure that Lamont was suspicious of him, but to his surprise, Jack didn't believe. Had he, Cliff would be at the bottom of the Sacramento River. Between him and Lamont, people were turning up missing all through town.

"I'm going to kill all those muthafuckas! Thinking they could come down here and run our hood," Marcus shouted.

Cliff looked out the window, nervous. "You need to lay low. With Kris and the rest of the squad being murked we are outnumbered. I thought they were on to me, but I was able to dodge that bullet. Let me make some more dough through them and then we bounce, come back and take over shit."

Listening to Cliff go over the plan, Marcus wasn't feeling leaving Sac, Sac was his town. How some out of towner's gon' run him out? Cliff was starting to sound like a bitch and why the fuck he got to lay low while Cliff getting his bread up? He wasn't feeling it and he didn't trust Cliff anymore. If he was willing to bite the hand that fed him, Marcus knew he would double cross him as well.

"If they want it, they can come get it. I'm not about to hide from no bitch or nigga. If I was in that hotel room, shit wouldn't have went down like that. You just stood there and let them kill the team," Marcus replied.

Glancing over at Marcus, Cliff was beyond furious. This fool had the nerve to be sitting up there acting tough, knowing that he was all talk and no action. Marcus had home from jail for only a few months.

Cliff shook his head, looking over to Marcus. "You do what you want, it's your funeral. And if I could've stopped them from offing the team, I would have. How you gone make it? How much money you have left?" When Marcus said nothing, Cliff knew he had proven his point. "Exactly!"

Thinking over what Cliff had just said, Marcus knew his words were were true. But to hide out made him look like a sucka. The cops had already found Kris and Snap, which wasn't the whole team, so it stood to reason that the police were going to come looking for him and Cliff next. When they'd left the pool hall the other night, it was the three of them. Now two were dead. He was so mad that he determined Jack and those bitches wouldn't know what hit them because he wouldn't rest until he got revenge for his people.

"Yeah, you might be right. But I tell you this, I'm gon' make sure all them bitches pay for what they did," Marcus said.

Cliff said, "What you thought, that they wasn't? I told you all that robbing them could mean life or death. Their crew may be run by women, but they're some of the most ruthless women I ever met."

Peeping the television at the news, Cliff saw that there was another killing the same night off of Garden Highway. The police had no suspects in custody and thought there was a serial killer on the loose. Neither Marcus nor Cliff noticed the picture of the man that was killed.

"Lay low, shit is going to look supicious if I don't show up to my post. I'll slide through later on tonight," Cliff said, handing Marcus an eight of purple and some cash.

Pulling off in his Lexus truck, Cliff stopped at the liquor store in the Manors for a bottle and a philly. As he cracked open the Hennessey, his phone vibrated. It was Jack asking where he was. Feeling a sense of relief, he relaxed a little knowing that Jack had no clue he was in on the robbery.

Driving down highway 5 feeling like a man who'd just won the lotto, Cliff exited W. El Camino and up to the trap house.

Walking over to the corner where Lamont and Monica were standing, Cliff said, "What's up? How shit moving today?"

"Shit is good, homie. Jack wants you to meet him at the main house," Monica replied.

Sitting in a chair in the trap house, overlooking the court, Jack noticed Cliff's car. He was so ready to bust at the nigga. He really had the nerve to show up smiling and shit. If there was one thing Jack didn't like, it was a snake ass nigga or bitch.

Alicia yelled from the kitchen, "Babe, Cliff is here!"

Strolling into the living room wearing the same shit from the night at the club, Cliff sat down and kicked his feet up on the coffee table.

"You look like shit and nigga, are you wearing the same shit from the club?" Jack inquired.

Cliff looked down at his clothes, "Yeah, I haven't even been to the house yet. I been shacked up with one of my little hoes."

"Hmm, well I'm switching shit up, you want be on the money anymore. I'm going to let you work the corner with Joe and watch him. Something's not right, there's a leak in the crew and were not sure who it is. But we'll soon find out. Do good out there and that may mean a promotion for you."

Cliff thought it over, "Man I don't know. Shit is hot and I'm not feeling being on the corner."

"I don't remember giving you a choice, my nigga. Either you can work the corner or you're out," Jack demanded.

Deciding it was best to let it go, Cliff said, "Alright, I hope we find out who it is so I can get back to what I am good at."

"Believe me when I say we will. A snake nigga or bitch will always have his day." Jack had gotten up and headed to the back leaving Cliff to think about what he'd just said.

Waking up to the sight of Alexis and Lamont and with her body hooked up to machines had Snow confused. She tried to speak but no words escaped her mouth and her arms felt like she had been lifting weights. Taking a deep breath, she focused on lifting her arm once more and was finally able to. That's when she patted Alexis on the head.

Feeling something touching her, Alexis looked up and smiled at the sight of Snow awake. "Hey Pooh your finally awake," Alexis muttered.

Snow tried to speak, her voice was squeaky and dry. "Where am I? What's going on?"

Lamont heard the commotion and woke up. "It's about damn time."

"Let me call the doctor in here and let them know you're woke," Alexis said, heading out to get a nurse.

Lamont strolled over to Snow's bedside and rubbed her face. "I'm glad you okay. It would've killed me if you didn't make it."

Looking up into Lamont's eyes, Snow saw sympathy and maybe something more. She hadn't noticed until now how handsome he was. Carammel skin with big brown eyes, not muscular, but also not skinny. He reminded her of Chris Tucker with a little more weight.

Lamont leaned in to give her a kiss on the cheek. Dr. Lee walked in and interrupted them by clearing his throat to let them know he had entered.

Gliding to the side so that the doctor could take a look at her, Lamont left the room to give her some privacy. No one knew it, but Lamont had a little crush on Snow. Unsure of what to do with those feelings and knowing Snow's background, he was hesitant to approach her. Sleeping in the chair for the last few days had his body aching, leaving her wasn't an option and now that she was okay he felt relief.

Checking Snow's vitals, Dr. Lee was impressed with the healing of her wound. He hadn't been so sure that she would make it with all of the blood she had lost. Even though she was sleep during the pain, the monitors indicated the pain her body had gone through. It was a lot more than she would have been able to handle.

"You're looking better than I expected after losing so much blood. How are you feeling?" Dr. Lee asked.

Snow smiled. "I'm in a little pain, but better pain than death."

"Is that transfer ready?" Alexis questioned.

"Yes. Now that she is awake, I feel a bit better about moving her," Dr. Lee confirmed.

"What's going on? Moving me?" Snow worried.

Alexis explained, "There's nothing to worry about, sis, we have to move you. A lot has gone down and we just want to make sure you safe."

"Where am I being moved to?"

Alexis hadn't thought about that and couldn't give Snow an answer. When she picked up her phone to text the girls for help in figuring things out, in walked Lamont.

He interjected, "Snow is coming to stay with me. She'll be cool, trust me, sis. Doc, get her ready."

Allowing her time to get it together, Lamont went back into the hall, called up his maid and let her know to get the guest room set up. He then sent out a text to the crew.

Lamont: She is awake, still in a lot of pain. Taking her to the underground. Will be out later."

Dr. Lee was holding the door open as Alexis rolled Snow out of the room in a wheel chair.

"I'll pull the car to the front door," Lamont advised.

Minutes later Lamont and Snow were heading down highway 5 while Alexis went home. Arriving there, Alexis had never been so happy to be home. She put the car in park and rushed inside. No one was awake yet due to it still being early and Alexis didn't have the energy to talk any way.

Making it to her room, she pulled out a t-shirt and went into her bathroom to run a hot bath. Pouring in some Johnson and Johnson calming bubble bath, she stepped into the tub. The moment her body hit the tub it relaxed and she enjoyed the feel of the hot water against her skin.

Chapter 15

For the last few weeks Red had been keeping her distance from the crew. She was in knee deep shit and there was no chance of changing what she had already done.

One night while on a date with a client, she fucked up and wasn't paying any attention. Sam, her date for the night, had laced her weed with some coke and she had been using ever since. A few months back, she and Cliff were running the spot and one thing led to another. The next thing she knew they were fucking on a regular basis and getting high together. Then things went from just kicking it to setting the crew up and she felt like shit about it.

When she wasn't high, all that was on her mind was making things right and confessing. But Red knew that if she told the crew the truth they would write her off or worse, they would kill her. Cliff had texted her during her date with a client, letting her know that shit went down and that that Kris and Snap were dead. For days Red was hiding out off of Watt at a cheap motel. That was the one place she knew they wouldn't come looking, especially after how horrible she told them it was being on the blade.

Her situation was just temporary until Cliff gave her the heads up that their cover had been blown. Then it would be time to leave town. Doing a line, she looked down at her phone to see if Cliff had hit her up. He had.

He'd sent a text that read: Shit is good, no one knows, come home lol!

Waking up to Christina pounding on her door, Alexis furiously opened it and walked back to her bed. "What the hell is wrong with you?"

"Something is not right with Red. Too many clients hit me saying they been inquiring about dates and Red hasn't gotten back to them." Christina complained.

Alexis replied, "Maybe she been busy. I'll talk to her."

"That's not it, I think Red is getting high, Lex." Christina confessed.

"Why you think that?"

Christina looked at Alexis like she had two heads and replied, "I know a fiend when I see one."

"Alright, let me check into it. Until we know what's up, she's no longer running POP Escort. You're up and give our customers a discount for the inconvenience. I just got in from the hospital and need some sleep, come get me once she makes it in," Alexis clarified.

Taking a quick shower and heading to the house, Red was ecstatic about being able to go back home. She thought she'd outgrown the raggedy ass motel and twenty bucks for head the tricks paid off of Watt. Once she made it to the house, she heard the television was blasting from the living room.

Red walked into the kitchen first and grabbed a water bottle. The coke had her mouth dry and the ecstasy pill had her grinding her teeth. She started drinking her water, staring out the window, daydreaming. She was startled by Christina who had been looking at her from the moment she entered the door.

Christina was sick of that bitch. She never trusted her and looking at her, she saw the reason why. From the beginning she felt like Red had snake ways and would be a problem.

"Oh shit, sis, you scared the shit out of me," Red said, holding her chest in shock.

Christina chuckled. "I scared you? You know this is a house full of women. And why you creeping anyways?"

"Creeping? I just rushed to the kitchen because I was thirsty, my date had me up all night," Red snapped back with a little attitude.

Walking away, Christina turned around and replied, "Alexis wants to talk to you."

Only having been given the job of running the girls for a few hours, already Christina had dates set up for the women. Word around town had spread so wide that Jordan had decided to open up another location to house the new recruits.

POP only housed the high class woman that men drooled over and no one was treated less than because of what they did. Most of the women looked at it as using what they had to make it. The opportunity they had been given was too sweet. There wasn't a man beating on them for all their dough, each girl received forty percent from each date, and no rent was asked of them. And to top it off, POP always treated them to the finest of places from hair salons to spas to the fact that their dates were nothing but gentlemen. Occasionally there were the weirdo's that like to be pissed on and beaten. Snow's motto was as long as they had that all mighty green, it was a go.

Red's room was downstairs. Going inside, she closed her door and locked it. Once safely tucked inside, she breathed a sigh of relief at being able to get out of eyesight of Christina. For some reason Christina never liked her. She played nice in front of everyone else, but when it was just the two of them she hardly uttered a word. Now Alexis wanted to talk to her and Red felt like a kid who'd just gotten caught by her parents.

With her high coming down, Red reached into her purse, took out her stash, scoped up some cream, and snorted.

Waking up in Isaac's arms felt like heaven. Finally able to sleep in and sleep in peace was what Jordan needed in her life. Lifting her head slightly, she opened her eyes and could tell it was later in the day. Isaac looked so peaceful that she didn't want to awake him. Plus she was still a bit tired and sore. All the love making from the previous night had put a hurting on her body.

Leaning in, she kissed Isaac on the crease of his neck and laid back down on his chest. Listening to his heartbeat and trying to drift back to sleep, her mind wandered to the crew and all they still had to accomplish. When they'd escaped Treasure Island, they had only one main enemy in mind. Asad. Now they had three enemies, three assholes on the loose.

"What are you thinking about?" Isaac startled Jordan from her thoughts.

Jordan smiled. "You, me, and the mess I have to fix."

"I want to thank you for opening up to me. It means a lot to me and after thinking about it a lot, I decided that I'm not going anywhere. These last few weeks without you have been tough," Isaac pointed out.

Jordan thought over what he said before speaking. "I'm glad you're sticking with me, it will be over soon."

"I don't know how I feel about you beefing with no nigga, though."

"I'm a big girl, I got it."

Isaac kissed Jordan on the forehead. "Well, I'm here if you need me, now get up off me so I can go piss."

Rising up, Jordan rolled onto her pillow, laid on her back, and grinned. Visualizing a future with that man made her feel joy. Hearing her phone vibrate, she reached over to the nightstand and took out her phone. There was a text message from Alexis.

Alexis: Sis get to the house, something not right with Red and we need to get to the buttom of it ASAP!!!

Frustrated, Jordan rose from the bed and headed into the bathroom. She had to use it and she wanted to let Isaac know there was a family emergency.

"What's wrong now, Jordan?"

Jordan replied, "Nothing is wrong. Alexis just texted, needing me to come home. You want to do dinner later?"

"I'm not tripping. It's going to have to be late, though, I have to get in the studio and prepare for my tour."

"Where's your next performance?"

"LA, next weekend. Why? You coming?"

"You bet your ass. I'll fly down, though, can't do the bus thing."

Disappearing into the room, Jordan pulled her hair into a bun. She then threw on her sweats, one of Isaac's shirts, and headed out the door.

Isaac rushed behind her and said, "Damn, no kiss or nothing?"

"My bad, boo!" Jordan walked back towards the door and leaned in, giving him a kiss.

Reaching into his pocket he handed her a key. "Next time, just let yourself in."

"I think that's a good idea. I'll do that and I'll just cook dinner tonight."

Isaac grinned, "Sounds like a plan to me."

The house where Isaac lived was in the cuts. There were many celebrities that lived in the community. Security there was tough because there were always groupies who would try sneaking in.

Pulling off in her car, Jordan looked in the rearview mirror and smiled at the sight of Isaac standing there in his basketball shorts with no shirt on. She thought about how fine he was, how his chocolate skin was so smooth. She thought about his light brown eyes that she could stare into all day and how that body of his made her wet just by brushing up against it.

Back at the house, Isaac reflected on how he wasn't the usual rapper who just spit that street shit, he was the rapper that actually lived it. He'd never introduced Jordan to that part of his life, thinking she would leave him. But to his surprise, he found that she came from a bad background too. The only difference was that hers wasn't by choice or by lack of good parents.

If she thought that he was gon' just stand by and let her take out that nigga by herself, she had another thing coming. It had been years since Isaac had let 4-5. his crazy alias, out. But if he was going to do it, why not do it now to defend his woman?

After Jordan pulled out of site, he went back into the house to retrieve his cell phone and dialed up one of his cousins in the Bay. As the phone rang, Isaac went into his closet and pulled out a pair of light blue vintage Levi's, a cream colored Polo shirt, his tan Timbs, and his piece.

"Damn, nigga, it's about time you answered. What the fuck you up to?" Isaac asked Jimmy.

Jimmy pulled the phone away from his ear to check the number. "Damn, nigga, long time no hear. I didn't know who the fuck this was."

"I'm sliding through to the town, you gon' be in the area?" Isaac asked.

Jimmy chuckled. "Of course, if you need me. Aww shit, who done pissed you off enough to bring out 4-5?"

"We'll talk about that in a minute."

Hanging up the phone, Isaac tucked his .45 in his stash spot hidden in the dash board of his 2014 Chevy Camaro. Smashing down highway 80 towards Oakland with YG blasting through the speakers, Isaac was on a mission to seek revenge on the man that destroyed a big part of Jordan.

Dreading having to talk to Alexis, Red went up the stairs to her room and was surprised how fast Alexis had brushed her off and told her they would be having a family meeting once Jordan came home. Alexis and the other girls were one thing, but Jordan had a low tolerance for bullshit and lies.

Trying to find out what the meeting was about, she was scared when she realized there was no such luck. Alexis rushed her out of the room. Figuring she had some time to kill and with her nerves was getting to her, Red went to the bathroom next to her room and took a shower. Shampooing her hair, she thought she heard someone's voice.

"Is someone there?"

No one said anything in response so she continued showering. Getting out of the shower and wrapping a towel around her hair, Red opened the door. There stood Jordan looking like she was ready for war.

Red said nervously, "Hey, sis!"

"Hey, didn't Alexis tell you about the important family meeting?"

Red peeked around Jordan to see if there was an audience. "My bad, I just needed a quick shower, my date had me up all night."

"I didn't know you had a date, my bad. Was it your regular John?" Jordan asked.

Red hesitated and then replied, "Girl you already know."

"A'ight, well come on, were all waiting on you," Jordan urged before going back into the dining room.

Shortly after returning to the dining room, Jack and Lamont arrived. Sitting at the table patiently waiting on Red, Christina placed the platters of food on the table. Tonight they were having meatloaf with green beans and homemade mashed potatoes.

"Well, it's about damn time," Jack barked towards Red.

Red cooed sarcastically, "I got dressed as fast as I could, damn. Sorry for washing my ass."

"Let's get down to business. It's been brought to my attention that POP hasn't been doing so well keeping the clients happy. Red, what's going on?" Jordan asked.

Taking a sip of water and trying to think of a good response, rep replied, "I've just been going through a lot and running the company. Plus keeping up with my own clientele is a lot."

"Un-hun. You said you were on a date with who last night?" Christina asked.

"John," Red replied.

Chrisitna looked at the list of clients she had spoken to and John, she remembered, was pissed "Red, you couldn't have been out with John, I've been on the phone with him all morning trying to calm him down. He needed a date for the banquet and no such luck."

"Let me see the nights count," Jordan instructed Christina.

Jordan handed the paperwork to Alexis and stood up to pour herself a drink at the bar.

"There's no way you were on a date with John. He is one of our most trusted clientele, he wouldn't lie about a date with you. So I'm going to give you one more chance to come clean," Alexis warned.

Looking around the room to see if anyone would come to her rescue, she quickly saw that no one would. All eyes were on her and they were all furious.

"Is this bitch gon' answer or just stare?" Alicia barked.

Pretending she was chocking, Red rose and went into the bathroom. Not far behind, Jordan watched her as she tried to figure her out. She wasn't the only one, though. They all had the same mentality, that Red was shady and up to something.

Christina shouted, "Bitch you need to bring your ass back in here and answer us."

Coming back to the dining room with her phone in her hand, she looked up and replied, "Damn if you must know, I have a friend I am seeing. I'm not sure where it's heading so I didn't want to tell any of you."

"Bitch, you a bold face lie, Sis, you gon' sit here and let this bitch continue to lie to our faces," Jack barked.

Alexis looked up. "I can't believe that after all we've done for you, you gon' sit here and lie to our faces. You didn't have shit and now you're rocking top designers."

"It's time for you to pack your shit and get the fuck out. I don't know what you're up to, but trust, were watching that ass," Monica said.

Before she could utter another word, Jordan held her hand up, "You're grimy, I knew it the moment I came and got you from your room. You sat there and lied like it was nothing. What happened to the love? Or appreciation? If I was you, Red, I would leave and I mean fast before I fuck you up."

Making her way back to her room, Red bent down beside her bed and pulled out a carrying bag. There was no way all her stuff would fit, but she had money and could purchase more shit. Throwing some clothes in the bags, a few pair of shoes and some other items, Red turned off the light and looked behind her before closing the door.

No one spoke a word to her as she left the house.

Power of the Pie

Chapter 16

Staying at Lamont's house had been too nice. Snow felt like she was on vacation and as the days drifted by, she was falling in love with Lamont. Prior to her being shot, they hadn't really talked much and he'd kept his distance from the women. Truth was, anyone who didn't know him, would think he was a rude ass hole.

Lamont had mad love from the streets, he'd started hustling in the streets of Sac at a young age. Not by choice, but because of the background he came from. The streets were a part of his upbringing.

His mother hadn't been the best in providing a stable environment. In elementary school, kids used to make fun of Lamont because of the things he wore and because of how often he wore them. By the third grade a teacher had taken a liking to him and taught him the fundamentals of life and of being a man.

Fifth grade came around and he went from slanging 8ths to pushing pounds. Jack and Lamont went way back to elementary.

When he got out of jail a few months ago, Jack looked out for him and put Lamont with the team.

From the first moment he laid eyes on Snow he wanted her, but his first priority was stacking his dough knowing that Snow wouldn't fuck with him if he stepped to her broke. Only being back in the game a few months had his paper game official.

Down in the kitchen he was making lunch for Snow. It had become their thing to sit, have lunch and discuss anything going on in the outside world. He could see Snow was getting better and soon would be ready to return back home.

Strolling in after taking a shower, Snow hadn't spoken a word and neither did Lamont. She grabbed the lemonade from the fridge and placed it on the table on the balcony. Sacramento weather was perfect to be outside that day. Taking in the sunlight, the two sat down and said grace before diving into their baked salmon, asparagus, and red potatoes.

"This meal is looking too good. Let me find out you're also a chef," Snow grinned.

Lamont looked up from his plate, blushing. "I'm any and everything you need, baby."

"Hmm, how many of your women you treat like this?" Snow asked.

His smiled disappeared. "I'm single, Snow, just got home not too long ago. My main goal is to stack my dough and get me a real woman by my side. If you stop playing, you can be the one."

"Don't get so upset, I was only playing. And you don't want to fuck with a woman like me."

"Why wouldn't I?" Lamont questioned.

Snow sighed, "I come with a lot of baggage, Corn, and I wouldn't want to put that on you. Or any other man for that matter. Plus, look at the kind of life we live. What kind of relationship can we build with that?"

"Snow, we all come with baggage. Does it look like your lifestyle bothers me? Shit, it actually does the opposite. I got respect for you and your girls, y'all doing your thing versus standing around with your hands out. Just give us a chance," Lamont pressed.

"Hmm, you ever dated a white girl before?"

Lamont laughed. "No, but that kind of shit don't matter to me. Just love me for me and always keep it a hundred."

"I can do that, it can't hurt to try. You know I been thinking it's time for me to make my way back home," Snow suggested.

"After lunch, pack up your things and I will take you."

After eating lunch, the two went to change and then they were off to Natomas to drop Snow off. Pulling onto the block of the house, Snow felt like a stranger. Lamont parked in the driveway, put the car in park and rushed over to the passenger side to help Snow get out the car.

"I wanted you to have this. I know this is your home, but remember you also have a second home with me," Lamont handed her a key.

Snow's eyes started to water up. "You are too sweet, what did I do to deserve you?"

After leaning in for a hug and a kiss, she entered the house only to be rushed by all of her sisters. Lamont stepped to the side and allowed the women their time. Each of them broke down into tears like it had been years instead of weeks.

Sariya broke up the group hug. "I missed you so much. Sis. It hasn't been the same without you."

"Damn, can a bitch get in the door?" Snow joked.

Walking into the family room, Snow sat on the couch and looked around. Everything was still the same as she remembered. One of the biggest, softest gray leather sectionals money could buy, with a purple and grey throw rug sat in the family room. The room was also filled with pictures of all the memories the women had created over the last year.

Staring at everyone, Snow noticed that there was only one person missing.

"I can't believe you all still watch this damn Love and Hip Hop, enough with these silly hoes already. Raine, what you over there doing in that computer?" Snow asked.

"Sis, you have to check out this website. The shit is crazy, it's something like a blog talking about these hoes on tv and topics about the things going on in the hood."

"What's the site?"

"Sskeepintitreal. It's pretty cool too, supposedly own by this black chick from the Bay!" Raine replied.

"I got it to check it out. Where is red?"

Taking a look at the women, Snow could sense something was wrong and decided to drop it for now.

Jordan interjected, "You just got home, go take you a bath and get some rest."

Snow agreed and headed up the stairs to her room. She had been so caught up in reuniting with her sisters that she hadn't noticed Lamont was gone. Opening her room door, she saw that the girls had redecorated her room with earth tone colors. Lying in the middle of the bed was a big ole stuffed bear. Alexis bought it for Snow knowing how much she loved him.

Running herself a hot bath, Snow stepped into the tub and relaxed. After being shot, her mind had gone into overdrive. The life she was living was not the she'd hoped to have as a child. Her childhood and dreams had been ruined because of that punk as nigga Asad and his sidekick Trent.

Lamont had tried to keep her from what was really going on in the streets. On some days she would listen in on his phone calls to Jack. She found out that Cliff was a snake, that he had set them up, and that some dude named Marcus was working with him. By the looks of Jordan though, Snow realized that something was up with Red as well.

1 week later...

To say Red was pissed was an understatement. At first when she was put out of the house and fired from POP, she assumed she would be okay. She figured the list of high rollers she had been able to obtain would keep her pockets fat and help her maintain.

Red had been staying at the house with Marcus. Cliff would come by every so often to check on them. For the first few days she didn't think anything of her regulars not calling her. By Thursday, though, she knew something wasn't right.

She picked up the phone to call John and he told Red he was no longer in need of her services. She was upset, told him to kiss her ass and to keep his little pocket change. Going through her contacts and calling more clients, she found that no one was answering her calls and the ones that did answer wasn't interested.

It was Saturday night, she was sitting in the empty, dirty ass living room thinking about how bad she had fucked up. Wiping away the tears that had sprang to her eyes, she went into the bathroom to wash her face. Red wiped her face with a towel, looked at herself in the mirror and began to feel rage as she wondered who the fuck did those hoes thought they were.

So what, she lied, but they had no proof. If they thought they were going to throw her to the streets and not feel her wrath, they had another thing coming. No one would reject her.

Her parents hadn't wanted her because she was the product of her mother being raped by her uncle. At a young age Red's mother put her out on the street and said she couldn't take looking at her any longer. Red had been on her own and when she met the girls, she

172

thought she'd found a family with POP. But no as soon as shit hit the fan, they threw her to the wolves. They would pay for that.

Hearing the front door open, Red made her way out of the bathroom to see if it was Cliff and if he had some blow with him.

"Damn, Red! What the fuck is wrong with you?" Cliff barked, looking like a bag of money.

Red checked out his swag and felt nothing but rage. "What's wrong with me? I'm trying to figure out how it's fair that Marcus and I are hiding out while you out there living the life. And how long you think it will take before they catch on to you?"

"First off, bitch, I don't answer to you or Marcus and secondly I don't plan on having them ever find out. It's not my fault you got caught slipping," Cliff barked.

Marcus allowed the two to hash shit out, but overhearing their argument got him to thinking about what Red said. It was time to put something in motion to avenge his homies and he knew just how he was gon' do it. It would be killing two birds with one stone.

Marcus cut in. "Check this out, it's time to make a move on them bitches, I'm done hiding out. You in or out?"

"Nigga, are you crazy! You barely walked out of the last situation with your life. Their out for blood and you already have a bounty out on your head," Cliff responded.

"Shit, I'm in. Those hoes got to pay, think they just gone throw me out and not pay," Red acknowledged.

Taking a glance at the two of them, Cliff shook his head, agreeing that he was in, but it was all a bluff. He was gon' stall them off for a few more weeks, just long enough for him to be on his way to ATL.

Cliff said, "Hell yeah, I'm down. What's the plan?"

"None of them knew that either of you set them up. Red, you need to try and work your way back in," Marcus suggested.

"They're never going to let me back in, they feel too strongly about loyalty and the fact that I lied. Jordan for sure is not having it." Red shook at that idea. She was lucky to have escaped with her life.

Cliff and Marcus were on the same page, but Cliff knew they would never let Red back in too. That was all Christina talked about at the trap, finding out what Red was up to and why she had lied. If the three of them could come up with a good plan, he might really get on board. Shit, it would be more money in his pockets.

"We'll think of something. Whatever we do, we gon' have to get ghost right after, though," Cliff affirmed.

Ordering up some Roundtable, the rest of the night was chill. Cliff knew what he was doing, he felt that if they stayed high enough they would let the shit go.

The blow had Red looking fucked up and she'd only been using for a few months. She was sexy as fuck, made other Asian broads mad. She had hair that went down past her ass with red highlights. She stood five feet, four with long, nice legs and breasts that sat up just right. And the things she could do with her pussy made a grown man moan like a bitch.

Checking her out, Cliffs dick got hard. He walked over to her and fondled her breast. Red didn't even care that Marcus was in the room, she pulled Cliff's dick out and started giving him head. Marcus looked at the commotion and unzipped his own pants, jacking off his seven inch dick. Marcus wanted in on the action so he made his way to the couch, pulling off Red's shorts. Taking a look at her nicely trimmed pussy, Marcus was eager to taste her.

"Eat that pussy!" Red hollered.

Taking a glimpse at Cliff's dick, Marcus was turned on by what he saw. The whole encounter was turning him on and had his dick hard to the maximum. Cliff noticed Marcus looking his way, the blow had him beyond high and horny.

Suddenly he took one of his hands and started stroking Marcus' dick. For a second Cliff was hesitant, that is until Marcus started giving him head. As Marcus was giving him head, Red got on her knees and started to suck Marcus' dick. Opening her legs while watching them, she played with her pussy.

Cliff took his other hand and started to play with Marcus' ass. At first Marcus tensed up, but then he relaxed. Cliff then inserted his finger in Marcus ass and Marcus began to moan, enjoying the sensation that was taking over his body.

Cliff got up and went into the bathroom, looking for something to lubricate his dick with. When he made his way back to the living room, he saw that Marcus was fucking Red from the back. Cliff put some baby oil in his hand and jacked off while watching the two. Going behind Marcus, he glided his hand back inside of him.

Marcus moaned, "This shit feel too good."

Cliff whispered in his ear, "When you get done, come back that ass up."

Marcus continued to work Red, then minutes later he pulled out his dick and squirted on her ass. Standing behind Marcus, Cliff kissed on Marcus' neck and stroked his dick. Going over to the couch, Cliff pushed Marcus down with his ass in the air. Cliff felt that Marcus was unsure so he got on his knees and began licking Marcus ass while jerking his dick. Marcus loosened back up and Cliff took that as an opportunity.

Lubricating his dick as his fingers re-entered Marcus' ass, Cliff stood to his feet and slapped his dick up against Marcus' ass. Opening his ass cheeks, Cliff glided his dick inside of Marcus little by little. Minutes later, he was all the way in.

After hours of them fucking and sucking on each other, they finally passed out and were only awakened by day light. Cliff woke up, looked around and was immediately ashamed of himself. He'd promised his self-years ago that he would never sleep with another man, but he'd broken that promise by sleeping with Marcus.

Gathering his clothes, he made his way to the bathroom, he was beyond upset. He wasn't gay, he loved women, but fucking Marcus felt too good. Cliff came to the conclusion that just because he enjoyed fucking a man didn't make him gay. I mean they weren't in a relationship, it was just sex.

Heading back to the living room, he looked at Marcus and became disgusted with himself.

For the last few days Isaac had been on the hunt to find out who the dude or the squad was behind all of the kidnapping. Jimmy had no information to give and ensured Isaac he would keep his ears to the streets. To say Isaac was under a lot of stress was an understatement.

Here he was getting ready to go on tour and Jordan had been bitching lately about his lack of time and affection. So tonight he decided to go all out for her and make her feel as special as the woman she was.

Isaac planned on taking Jordan away for the weekend to a bed in breakfast in Napa.

"Where are we going?" Jordan asked as they drove down highway 80.

Isaac ignore her nagging, he threw in his Lil Wayne Carter cd and hit the blunt.

"I know you hear me. Where are we going?"

Isaac turned down the radio. "Ma, just sit back and chill. I got you."

Exiting Novato, they drove fifteen more minutes down the highway and made it to their destination which was in the middle of wineries. Jordan, still confused about what they were doing there, she got of out the car and followed Isaac inside.

The desk attendant asked, "How can I help you?"

"Isaac Harris checking in."

"Hello, Mr. and Mrs. Harris. I have your room all set up. Here is your itinerary for the weekend," the desk attendant ushered them up the stairs.

Opening the door, Jordan was awestruck. The room was filled with rose petals, wine, and chocolate covered strawberries.

"Omg! When did you plan this? I thought you forgot about me," Jordan walked in scanning the room.

Isaac smiled, "Don't worry about all that, I could never forget about you. I need you to remember that. I got you, ma, you just got to trust me and ease up on a nigga. I'm about to go down to the car and get our bags."

Sitting on the bed, Jordan started thinking to herself, This man is the one, he really loves me for me and I love him. Her mind drifted to the possibilities of things between them not lasting if he ever found out the truth. Would he still love me if he knew I ran a drug empire?

"Why are you still sitting there with your jacket on?" Isaac inquired.

Jordan was pulled from her train of thought. "I was waiting on you to come undress me."

"You haven't said nothing but a word boo."

Isaac put the bags down and went into the bathroom to run them some bath water. Removing his clothes, he called for her to come into the bathroom with him. Jordan walked in and adored the man who stood before her. His chocolate skin was so smooth, his hair was nicely trimmed and his dick was standing at full attention.

The scent of Gucci Guilty lingered in the air. Isaac's body was the perfect build, it drew her end and his stare demanded her attention. Gazing into his eyes, Jordan removed her clothes, no words needed to be spoken. Each had a lot on their mind and some time to themselves was needed.

Completely undressed Jordan, Isaac held out his hand and guided her into the water. Lying in the tub against Isaac's chest, Jordan took a deep breath and exhaled.

"So tell me what's been going on, my queen?"

Jordan sighed. "Something is up with one of the girls, we had to cut her. She was lying about her whereabouts, but the problem I'm having is I think it's more to her than just lying."

"Did she cause any problems when you cut her off? And more to it, like what?"

"She is new to the team so of course her loyalty is in question, but she had been cool, up until a few weeks ago. I just don't want to push it to the back and it becomes a problem for us."

Isaac advised, "Trust your gut. If something don't seem right, then check into it. If it turns out she's a snake, dead the bitch."

Turning around in shock of Isaac's reaction, Jordan didn't know if she should be turned on or worried. Isaac never came off as a square, but never a killer either.

"Damn, babe, you not playing. What's gotten into you?" Jordan was a bit disturbed.

Isaac chuckled. "Jordan, there's a lot about me you still have to learn. I'm from the streets, the shit I rap about I lived. No fronting over here."

After an hour of soaking in the bathtub, the two were plastered in front of the fireplace sipping on red wine.

Awakening the next morning to a knock at the door letting them know the tour of the winery will be leaving soon, they immediately got up and got dressed. By the end of the day they were woren out and tipsy from all the wine they indulged in.

For the remainder of the weekend they stayed in their room with their cell phones off and relaxed. For Isaac, the trip solidified their union and given them the chance to learn more about one another.

Chapter 17

Since Red has been gone, POP was back up and running. Christina was waiting on her turn to show her worth within the company. Some were still running on edge knowing Marcus was still somewhere out there.

It ate Jack up knowing Cliff was a snake and having to smile in his face was torture. Jack put Cliff on the block to keep him out of the loop and out his face before he wound up killing his ass. Word got back to the connect about the beef stirring up in Sac and that had the bosses a little weary.

Lost in a train of thought while watching the knocks being served, Jack was interrupted by a text message from Alicia.

Alicia: Hey, babe, I'm on my way to the spot. You need me to bring anything?

Jack replied: Yeah, some of that pie, lol.

Alicia: You don't have to tell me twice! ☐

Just was Jack was about to reply back when Cliff walked in looking dumb as fuck. He was sporting every name brand Nordstrom's had in their stores.

"Damn, why you got on all that flashy shit to work the block?" Jack asked, breaking up a swisher.

Cliff looked down at his clothes and smiled. "It's nothing. I work hard so I can spend even harder."

Jack shook his head and turned his back to Cliff as he looked into the courtyard. Money was moving, the nocks were happy, and things couldn't be any better.

"How much longer am I going to be working the block?" Cliff asked.

Jacked turned around with his face frowned up. "What, nigga, you not eating? Your pockets empty?"

"Naw, it's not that, but I been down with the team for too long to be still slanging on the corners. I proved my worth in the beginning, I'm trying to be back on the money," Cliff nagged.

Jack looked Cliff in the eyes and said, "It's like this, everyone on the team is looked at differently after we got hit. You proved your worth but let me ask you this, did you prove your loyalty?"

"I think so. I been down with the squad since day one," Cliff gloated.

Jack snickered. "Like I said, we don't know who we can trust and until the snake is revealed, you're on the block."

Going back outside clear of Jack, Cliff went to his corner pissed. Who the fuck did Jack think he was? And why was he the only one being treated any differently?

On the block with the new worker, Gene, Cliff said, "Man, fuck this shit. Got us out here in this hot ass weather nickel and diming while they up there with the AC kicked back."

Gene laughed. "Damn, what's gotten into you?"

"It don't bother you that you're on this corner sweating while they're kicked back up top?" Cliff pointed to the trap house.

Gene thought it over and replied, "Nope. Because they pay me cool and every nigga on their team has been promoted. Well, everyone but you."

"Yeah, whatever nigga. My day coming soon, believe that. Or it's going to be some bloodshed." Cliff responded, not thinking before he talked.

Alicia pulled up to the spot wearing some tight, white 7 For All Mankind shorts with a silk, pink spaghetti strapped shirt that was cut low enough to reveal her nice size D breasts. As she hopped out of her 2014 GT Mustang, the men passing by began to whistle.

Alicia had the kind of beauty where nothing was needed and Jack preferred her like that , he wasn't into all the makeup. The one thing she wasn't willing to give up was her weave. Alicia loved her some Jack, however, cutting out her weave was not happening.

Since spring was lurking around the corner, she changed her hair color to a light brown with blonde highlights. She usually wore it curly, but today she went bone straight with some loose curls at the bottom. The blonde and brown brought out her caramel complexion and her light brown eyes.

Watching her walk across the yard with some lunch for Jack, Cliff asked her to come here for second. Cutting her eyes, she thought, I can't believe this silly muthafucka is still here. Can't wait for the opportunity to murk his ass.

Stopping to talk to Cliff before going in, Alicia said "What's good Gene? Cliff, what's up?"

"Shit, you? You looking right in them shorts. What you got for daddy in them bags?" Cliff flirted.

Alicia shook her head. "Why, thank you! And you want to know what I have in this bag? I got my daddy some lunch and something to go with his desert."

Turning up his face to her reaction and feeling like shit because Gene just witnessed him being clowned by this broad, he looked away from her as she walked away.

"That shit not funny, youngster. If she wasn't fucking with Jack I could've tap that," Cliff revealed.

"That's what would've never happened. You are not her type and why you rambling so much about Jack? You starting to sound like a hater," Gene replied.

Opening up the door to the trap house, Alicia sat the bags that were filled with their lunch down on the table and started to unpack their food so they could eat. Strolling up behind her, Jack put his arms around her waist and kissed on her neck.

"What you think you're doing with these little ass shorts on?" Jack asked.

Alicia's pussy was soaked just from his touch. She cooed, "These old things. You like them, hun?"

"Hell yeah. Let me see what this shit be like," Jack whispered in her ear as he unbuttoned her shorts and put his hand down her pants.

Alicia tried to play hard to get and act like she was so concerned with their lunch getting cold. "Babe, that can wait. I don't want our food to get cold."

"Shut up and enjoy this shit! You don't like it?"

"Nope."

Jack responded, "You a lie! This pussy is soaking wet for a nigga."

Pulling her shorts all the way down, his dick became hard. Alicia wasn't wearing any panties, which turned him on even more. Jack only had on some basketball shorts and he quickly took them off and glided his dick on her ass. Alicia knew what time it was. She bent over on the table and played with his dick with her left hand.

"You see how much Danger been missing this good pussy," Jack said in a low voice.

Alicia let out a moan and demanded, "Stop playing and make this pussy talk."

While he was in the act of him entering her, she let out a gasp as if the intake of his dick gave her the ability to breathe again. Every time Jack fucked Alicia or made love to her it was like they were one and he knew exactly how to give her the dick.

She hollered, "Nut in this pussy, Jay!"

Throwing the pussy back at him before somebody walked in a ruined their session, Alicia began squeezing her pussy muscles around his dick. Then she took one of her hands and played with herself. Shit had been so stressful for the crew, it started to put a dent in their relationship. The two rarely saw each other. Unless it was at the trap house.

Rained hated to admit it, but Alexis had right about Asad. The moment his boys started coming up missing, he wanted to get away for a little bit. He told Raine it was to ease his mind, but in reality he was shaken up and couldn't help but to think he was next.

Sitting at the house, waiting for the gang to arrive for their Sunday family dinner and meeting, Raine took it upon herself to get dinner started. She was tired of soul food and decided to make Gumbo. Cleaning the crabs, her mind started to wander on her finding love like her sister. She was ready to be done with the whole Asad business and find herself a real nigga. If only Asad was as real as he pretended and not such a creep. Aside from her disliking what he did for a living, Ranie was falling for him hard and Asad was falling for her.

Walking into the kitchen, Monica said, "What's up, sis! What you over there thinking hard about?"

"Girl, life and ready to find me a boo," Raine responded.

"I hear you there! All these chicks running around here in love and shit," Monica joked.

"Right! That's alright, with all we been through, we all deserve nothing but the best," Raine advised.

The two continued to clean the crabs and prepare the gumbo. Monica went into her purse, pulled out her iPhone and put on some Mary J. Blige for them to jam to. While they were blending up the tomatoes, Raine phone went off. It was Asad texting her again about going away with him for a few days. She replied and told him she would let him know by the end of the night.

"Hmm, someone putting a smile on that face. Let me know you got a boo," Monica teased.

Raine blushed. "Not at all. That's Asad's ass acting scared since his people getting killed. I'm so ready for this meeting to start, the shit is starting to stress me the fuck out."

Before Monica could give Raine some advice, Snow walked into the room and began helping with dinner. The last week for Snow things had been back to normal and she missed it. Knowing there was still something's she was left in the dark about, tonight she was going to get to the bottom of it. Yes, she was shot, but she wasn't a child, she was a big part of POP. Time went by and once dinner was served all was accounted for.

Sariya stood up to give grace. "Let's all bow our heads. Dear, Heavenly Father, thank you for ensuring we all made it here tonight safe and sound and for bringing our sister Snow home to us. And bless the hands that prepared this meal. Please let this food be nutritious to our minds, bodies and souls. In Jesus' name we pray, amen."

Soft melodies were playing in the background as they ate their gumbo and chatted a bit. Each woman was eager to get on with things and discuss business.

"I'm glad you all could make it tonight. As you all know, the supplier isn't happy about the street beef we have going on. They're worried that people think were soft because our shit was hit. We have an emergency meeting with the bosses and I'm hoping shit goes cool. Jack, any word on Cliff and Marcus?" Jordan asked.

Jack replied, "Naw, sis. I'm ready to take this nigga Cliff out, he had the nerve to complain about working the corner."

"I heard the fuck up out of that," Alexis mumbled.

Snow jumped in. "Okay, I'm confused and need to be brought up to date. I'm trying to figure out why Red was put out and what's going on with Cliff?"

Jordan raised her hand to break the news to Snow. "First, Red was running the escort side as you know and came back pretending to have gone on a date. We found out she was lying and clients haven't been served in weeks. When we all approached her, she denied it and continued to lie. You know how we feel about disloyal muthafuckas."

"Okay. She lied, but why?" Snow asked.

Jordan chuckled. "Sis, I'm so glad you're back. You're thinking like me, why would she lie? Something's not sitting right with me and this whole situation."

"Hmm, now what about Cliff? And who the fuck is Marcus?" Snow questioned.

"Marcus was one of the dudes that hit the trap house and Cliff set the whole thing up," Lamont pointed out.

Christina shot up "Oh, Shit!"

"What?" Everyone chimed in.

Christina urged, "You think she was in on setting us up? I mean her and Cliff worked the trap house together."

"I bet money that's what it is," Alicia agreed.

Sariya barked, "Scandalous ass bitch. I'm gon' murk her snake ass."

"Damn, she know so much about our operation, where we live, everything," Monica pointed out.

Raine went to the bar and brought back some Henn. "We have another problem. Asad wants me to go out of town with him. I don't know about that."

"Go where?" Sariya asked.

Raine replied, "I'm not sure, he didn't say."

"Well, we don't want him to become suspicious and fuck up our plan. Snow and Lamont will go with you, but he won't know that. They'll go just to have your back and in case shit goes bad," Jordan suggested.

Snow implied, "I thought we had a meeting with the bosses, sis."

"Alexis and I can handle it. I need you to watch Raine's back," Jordan recommended.

"What about Cliff and them?" Sariya was worried.

Lamont raised his hand to speak. "It's time for y'all to pack it up and move elsewhere. It's too risky with Red out there and working with Cliff."

It would be hard saying goodbye to their first home away from Treasure Island. Lamont was right, though, it was a bittersweet. By the end of the meeting some of them felt a bit more at ease. Jordan suggested they recruit more soldiers and hook up with the connect for more artillery.

With Joshua now dead, Asad realized that he wasn't on one and that his squad was under attack. He was beyond happy that Zariya, as he knew her, agreed on going with him. Although he wanted to leave the following morning, Zariya told him that she had to put in a two week notice before a trip.

Sitting in his office, Asad browsed the internet, checking out the perfect location for him and Zariya. The prices were ridiculous due to the fact that he booked the flight and resort at the last minute. Scrolling on Orbitz.com, he decided that a cruise to the Bahamas would be perfect. The boat docked in LA which was perfect. They would be able to drive down and shop for a few hours before sailing out.

Tonight, the new recruitment of girls had just arrived, business had been booming for Asad. Now that he had another worker out, he was gathering up more solders to be on the squad. It wasn't easy, not too many men were okay with pimping and kidnapping. They were afraid of the charges that it came with and the things they did to men who went down for rape or molestation was brutal.

Making his way to the main border house, Asad took in the sun shining and wished he was somewhere off with Raine giving her the dick. He smiled at the thought of the last time he hit it.

Rounding up people to work at Treasure Island was moving too slow for Asad. He needed men who weren't afraid to get their hands dirty. Opening up the door, Asad looked around at all the beautiful women that stood before them. Some were crying and others just stood still and silent.

Asad barked, "Listen up, this is your new home. If you're even thinking about escaping, let me be the first to tell you that it will never happen. Do as you're told and things don't have to get ugly."

The whole routine was getting old to Asad. It wasn't about the money for him, it was all about the control and the fear he instilled in those women. Ten woman stood in front of him and none aroused him. Each stood there naked, using their hands to cover up their exposed areas. It tickled Asad because those woman would soon be sold off to the highest bidder and make him a rich man.

Looking over the girls, his mind drifted to the ones that got away and he wondered where they were. Could they be behind killing of my team?

Asad yelled, "If you're related or any of the girls standing beside you, raise your hand?"

Two of the woman raised their hands, giving notice that they were related. Asad divided the two and planned on keeping them apart.

He didn't want any of those women to feel a sense of comfort and having a relative with them could make them feel like they could accomplish anything. Like escaping. That's where he knew he failed when it came to Jordan and Alexis. Two bold women held captive for years. His mistake allowed them the opportunity to plan and escape.

"Gentlemen, let's get these ladies ready. I have some new clients coming to visit tonight," Asad ordered.

Dividing the women into groups by age, size, and color, he realized that the batch wasn't the best he'd ever laid eyes on, but after his glam squad was finished with them, they would be presentable to any man's eye.

Only three men were still standing in the room once, one in which was the newest and youngest to the team. He liked Jakar, though, he was young and dumb. Always fast to pull out them thangs and get shit poppin'.

"So as you three know we have been under attack for the past few weeks and have lost some good people. I'm starting to think the people behind this are the women that escaped some months ago. We need to track them down," Asad suggested.

Jakar snickered. "You think a woman can get down like that? I mean, Joshua wasn't a nigga that easy to take out. He was always on his shit."

Asad turned towards the youngster. "I'm not sure about that, but I do know one thing for sure, though, I don't want to assume their not behind this and lose more men."

"How would we go about finding them?" Eric asked.

"Let's start with social media, Facebook and Instagram," Asad recommended.

After giving the information they needed to find the women who disappeared, Asad got to thinking about the torture he would make each feel. Breaking him from his thoughts, Asad received a text message from Zariya.

Zariya: Hey, boo. I can't wait to go away with you and get some of that dick. Where are we going anyway?

Asad: The Bahamas, on a cruise. We dock from LA, so we can drive down there. I cant wait to give you this dick lol.

Twenty minutes went by before Zariya responded: I'm too excited, I never been before, let me get my two pieces ready lol. So we're leaving that Friday?

Asad: Yes, ma'am. Two weeks to get everything straight over there."

Zariya: Got it! I already put in my request at work. Hit me when you get off babe!

Asad shot back: Will do.

Making his way back to his office, Asad thought about how Zariya came into his life at the perfect time. Maybe it was time to shut shit down and just enjoy life. He had more than enough dough stacked to live good and comfortable for the rest of his life.

Chapter 18

For the last few days Red had been back working the blade off of Watt. She was done relying on Cliff to come through with some coke and what she witnessed between him and Marcus made her look at them both differently. They both had been so drugged up that they hadn't notice she was staring at them the whole time. She wasn't as surprised by Cliff, but Marcus came off a little more hard core.

Standing on the corner where cars exited the freeway and trying to flag down a trick, Red noticed Christina's silver, LX450 and in the car with her was Snow. Pretending she didn't see them, she rushed across the street and into the Starbucks bathroom.

Locking herself in there, she stayed for a good twenty minutes before someone came knocking on the door. Back outside, Red glanced around and didn't see the car any longer. However, when she turned the corner, to her surprise, there stood both women, dressed to impress.

Snow was wearing a long summer dress with her hair in a messy bun and curls falling to the front. Christina was rocking all-white skinny leg True's, a white True Religion shirt, and the retro blue 11 Jordan's.

"Damn, sis, if I didn't know any better I would think you were hiding from us," Snow half joked.

Christina laughed and said, "Red, why you hiding from us?"

"I'm not hiding, I had to use the bathroom," Red stuttered.

Snow responded. "What's this I hear about you lying to your sisters? I thought we were family and after all we've done for you."

"I didn't lie. It's not my fault you all don't believe me," Red shot back, agitated.

Christina snickered and walked a bit closer to Red. "Damn after all that we have done for you, you do us like this. You gone stand in our faces and still lie. I just want you to know that I never trusted your scandalous ass and I'm looking for a reason to put a hot one in you."

"All you have to do is be honest and you can come back home, we all know you're not getting no money out here. Not like you use to at POP. What you making a hundred a day maybe?" Snow questioned.

Thinking it over, she decided that whether she chose to be honest with them or not, she had nothing to lose? Hun, her life. Fuck that, even if I tell them, they're still going to kill me for setting them up.

Red looked them both over before walking off. "I'm making it, I'll be okay."

Looking both ways before she crossed the street, Red was disgusted with herself and the position she put herself in. Snow was right, she went from being a something to a nothing overnight, back to where she was, selling her pussy for chump change. Standing on the corner contemplating if she would regret telling them the truth, snickering to herself, I would be a damn fool.

Snow was in disbelief of what her eyes had witnessed. Red looked worse than when they'd first met her. Snow was unsure of how she should feel about Red. One side of her was upset and the other side felt sad for Red.

Just by looking at her you could tell she was on drugs. Red had only been away from home for a few days and already the weight had dropped. Parked across the street from where their former sis was working, they sat in Starbucks' parking lot in the hopes that she would lead them to Marcus and Cliff hideout.

"Sis, this bitch looks hella dumb out here," Christina complained.

Snow turned up her nose, not feeling how Christina was so cold towards Red "Shit is hard out here, if it wasn't for Jordan taking them keys and Alexis hooking up with the connect, there is no telling where we would be. I'm not feeling her lying and if she set us up, her day will come sooner than she thinks."

"It's like this, I got much love for her, I'm just not willing to allow no one else knock us down. Asad was the last person to fuck us over and that's my word," Christina confessed.

Daylight turned into night too fast, but Red still stood out on the corner trying to get a date. Finally realizing it wasn't going to happen, she headed down towards the bus stop. Christina had dozed off and was pissed off when Snow woke her up to let her know Red was on the go.

Pulling behind the bus, the two followed it, but not to close where she would notice the car. Thirty minutes later they wound up in some raggedy ass neighborhood where Christina's car stuck out like a sore thumb. It was giving them more attention than they expected.

Exiting the bus and walking towards the house, Red noticed the dudes looking past her. Turning around to see what caught their attention, she was surprised that the back of a Lexus, but she wasn't sure not sure who's. Continuing on her way to the house, she walked inside and found Marcus sitting in front of the television.

"What's wrong with you?" Red asked.

Glancing up from the television, he replied, "Shit, just tired of being in this house. You want to go hit up a bar or something before I lose my mind?"

Shaking her head, red went into her room to get something to change into and to take a shower. There were a few under spots they could go to without being spotted.

Days went by, they still had nothing on Marcus' whereabouts and Cliff had yet to slip up. Jack and Lamont had been on him like a hawk and to their surprise he had the same routine, to the club and off to the motel with some thot.

The pressure was more on Jack than on anyone. He felt it was his fault that Cliff set them up and that it may cost them. As they were parked outside of the motel, Jack got a text message from Christina.

Christina: Bruh, one was found but now she is lost. Too many eyes, but we will make our rounds back.

That was good news. Snow and Christina were able to find Red, but lost track of her. It was just an assumption that Red was in on things with Cliff and if it turned out that it was true, she was going down with the snakes.

Alexis, Snow, and Jordan were on their way to San Diego to meet the bosses and each woman was nervous. They came into this game new and unaware of the dangers that came along with getting dough and taking over someone else's spot. Snow had called for the meeting now, before she headed to the Bahamas. Like hell she wasn't going to be a part of this meeting.

Alexis exited the freeway to grab a bite to eat and to ensure that they each were on the same page going into this meeting.

Once they were seated in IHOP, Alexis said, "Are you two worried?"

"Worried about what?" Jordan asked.

Snow chuckled. "All we need to do is make sure they know we have things under control and are taking care of the loose ends."

"Right, I mean it's not like we have been late or short of our dough," Jordan agreed.

Alexis mumbled, "Do you think we're in over our heads?"

"Not at all. We came into this game wet behind the ears and struggling. Now look at us, more money than we can count and respect everywhere we go. We just fucked up trusting the wrong people," Jordan acknowledged.

"I guess you're right. Let's get this meeting over with, handle the three stooges, and get back to living," Alexis suggested.

Snow ate a bite of her pancakes and said, "If you two would've seen Red, I mean the girl looked bad. You can tell she has something to hide. When we followed the bus and she got off, she continued to look over her shoulder. Of course we had to get ghost in that hood with the Lexus, they was on us."

"I want her dead as well. She crossed us and knows too much to let her just walk. Are you two willing to go to jail? Because that is a possibility. On top of everything else, she knows we going after Asad. She could easily start running her mouth," Jordan implied.

"I agree," Snow replied.

Alexis thought about it and without a second thought, said "We need to shut that shit down ASAP."

Picking up her glass of orange juice, Jordan raised it to solidify what they'd just agreed to. Only an hour away from San Diego, Jordan drove the rest of the way and threw in her K. Michelle cd. Alexis and Snow drifted off to sleep and as they slept Jordan got to thinking about how far they'd come.

In her eyes they were exactly where they belonged and wasn't so sure she wanted out. Of course the life of a wife and mother was something her heart yearned for but just not right now. The questioned that lingered in her mind was how Isaac would look at her if he found out. Sooner or later she would have to tell him and deal with the outcome.

After their weekend in Napa, Isaac opened up to her and allowed her to know him. For that she owed him honesty. Learning that her man use to be the man and he could hold his own made Jordan more than sure he was the one for her. Isaac trusted her with his skeletons and she could do the same with him.

Pulling up to the valet at the Marriot, Jordan saw that Snow and Alexis were still sleep. She went inside to check them in and to get the bags checked in. She was treated like VIP whenever she came into town, the manager knew she had money and wanted to keep the girls happy. Every time there was a trip made down to San Diego, the Marriot is where they would stay.

Walking up to the front desk Jordan said, "Hey, Joseph. We're checking in."

"Hello, Mrs. Grant, here are your keys. I expected you all a lot later. I hope you enjoy your stay with us. Should I send the usual up?" Joseph asked.

Jordan looked around the lobby and replied, "Sure, two bottles of champagne this go around."

Proceeding back to the truck, Jordan nudged Alexis and Snow, notifying them that they had arrived at their destination. By the time they made it to the room, there was breakfast and mimosa's waiting.

After eating and throwing back a few mimosa's, Jordan got in the shower and changed into some True Religion jeans, a silk white shirt and some seven inch peanut butter Aldo heals. She pulled her hair up in a messy pony tail with nude make up on her face. Jordan's appearance screamed sexy, but also professional.

Alexis' hair flowed down her back in nice soft curls. She wore a black, long sleeve maxi dress, that cascaded down to her knees with some black ankle boots. Today she was going with the look of a bitch not to be fucked with. Yes, they were beefing in the streets, but money had doubled in the last few weeks and POP ensured that none of the beef came there way.

For Snow, this meeting was her time to show to the bosses that she was still in control. Yeah, she took a bullet. To some, they thought it would slow her down but it did just the opposite. Before, on nights when she was laid up with strange men, she felt like her life had no purpose and it wasn't until that very moment she knew what her destiny was. She was mean to be a boss bitch.

When Jordan made the suggestion of taking out Red and stressed the point of Red being a threat to the family, without a second thought she knew what had to be done.

Standing in front of the mirror, Snow wiped it to get a better look at herself. She was more than satisfied with what she saw. She was wearing some white slacks that hugged her hips just right with a hot pink, silk shirt and pink Prada pumps . Her hair was in a high bun and she wore little to no make-up.

Throwing on her Gucci shades, Snow went into the room and said, "You two ready."

Jordan stopped texting Isaac, checked out Snow from head to toe and smiled. Her sister was back. To a stranger those woman looked so different, on the inside, though, they were the same only birthed by different mothers. But they lived with the same heart and the same mind frame. To kill or be killed was there motto.

While Jordan was out of town, Isaac had a few small events he had to perform at. Nothing big, just a few clubs to show his face and reach out to his fan base. It was amazing how fast the music industry accepted him and his music. One thing he promised himself when getting into the business was to always stay true to his fans.

Sometimes when artists got into the industry they were selling wolf tickets and people were buying. They were rapping about money, hoes, and the material shit they had, but in reality those niggas were living with their moms or barely making it. 4-5 received so much love from the people because he kept it real. What he rapped about, he actually lived and made it out.

Tonight he was at a club off J St. called Tap Out and the club was overcrowded with people. To Isaac, this type of crowd wasn't a surprise. He couldn't help but to think about Jordan as he sat in his VIP section scanning the audience.

Taking a shot of Patron, Isaac noticed Jasmine and her ratchet ass friends. He smirked to himself at the thought of the confrontation at his house between Jordan and her.

Jasmine noticed Isaac checking her out and decided to walk over to the VIP. She tried to barge in but was stopped by Isaac's security. "Damn, Shawn, you gone do me like that. A bitch can't get in!"

"Let her in, Shawn," Isaac ordered.

Jasmine smirked and walked past him. "Hey, handsome, how you been?"

"I been chilling, how about yourself?" Isaac smiled, showing off them pearly whites.

Jasmine sat down and crossed her legs. "How did we get here, 4-5? I thought we were building something."

"Shit, I don't know why. I told you what shit was from the get and you allowed your feelings to get in the way," Isaac shot back.

"Sometimes we can't control what we feel. I knew you had just got out of a relationship, but you can't blame a girl for trying." Jasmine was just about to give him an ear full about how scandalous he was for allowing Jordan to come at her the way she did. But as she was opening her mouth to continue, her new friend Red walked up and introduced herself.

"Hey, girl. I been looking for you and your ass up here cup caking in VIP," Red was irritated.

Jasmine looked from her to Isaac. "My bad, girl come sit down for a sec. Isaac, this my girl, Red, Red Isaac."

Red held out her hand. "Nice to meet you, Isaac. Your music is on point. If you ever need a model for one of your video shoots again, I'm your girl."

"What's good, Miss Red? Long time no see. You know I leave that part up to J," Isaac confessed.

Red became envious. "I guess. Where is your girl? I'm surprised she let you out alone?"

"Don't worry about that, she don't have nothing to worry about. I'm working and so is she," Isaac barked.

Red mumbled, "If that's what you call it."

Isaac started to get upset and knew it was best if he excused the ladies from his VIP. "Well, it was nice to see you ladies. You both have a good night and be safe out in these streets."

"Damn, it's like that? A bitch can't kick it with you for the night?" Jasmine asked.

"Naw, ma, it ain't that kind of party. I have a lady and you and I are the past," Isaac gestured for them to leave.

Jasmine got up. "You just let your bitch know that I'll be seeing her in the streets for the little shit she pulled."

"Bitch, is that a threat? Jasmine, I think it's best if you call it a night and think twice before you think I'm gon' let you come for what's mine. I'm gon' let that threat go for now. Shawn, escort these two out of the club, please," Isaac said, ready to snap that bitch's neck in two.

Jasmine caused a scene. "Nigga, you don't own this club, I'll leave when I'm good and ready," she shouted.

There were no more words that needed to be spoken. Shawn did as he was told and put Jasmine and Red out. For a second Red was going to jump in and have Jasmine's back, but fuck that. She knew first-hand how Jordan took to threats.

When the Jasmine and Isaac were arguing back and forth in the club, Red knew the look Isaac was wearing all too well. It was the look of death and she was almost certain that if it had been just them three in the spot, she and Jasmine would've been six feet under.

Departing the parking garage in Jasmine's Buick, Isaac's ex was still pissed off at Isaac and going on about how she was going to get payback. Red shut her out and had started thinking about hitting POP. If Jordan was out of town, that meant Alexis and Snow was with her. Those three was the most lethal in the crew.

"Bitch, do you hear me? I'm gon' fuck your ex girl up," Jasmine hollered.

Red replied, "Shit, I don't give a fuck, I'm over here thinking about going to shoot up their shit. Bitches crossed me and you, let's do this," Red suggested.

"I'm down, but we not gon' just shoot their shit up, they have too much dough. We need to rob their asses and be ghost," Jasmine added.

Red thought it through and smiled. There was always a cool stash at the house and more than enough to take and be out.

"This could work. They have a few hundred grand at the house, we're going to need to include Marcus and Cliff," Red recommended.

Jasmine wasn't feeling that. "Fuck that! All four us can't eat off that."

"Don't let the fact that Jordan is a female fool you, she will kill you and not think twice about it. Going in there with just us two, we wont make it out alive. Some money is better than nothing."

Jasmine shook her head in agreement. "True. Let's do it, I am down. I'll figure out a way to get Isaac back as well."

Being dropped off at the corner on Watt, Red waited for Jasmine to pull off before she headed home. Jasmine and Red became friends just out of nowhere. Red had gone to the club with Marcus, to some little hole in the wall off Watt, and Jasmine was there with this old school pimp. Jasmine was feeling Marcus and with one shot after the next, they all found themselves at a motel fucking on each other.

When Jasmine got home, she ran the idea down to Marcus and he was down. Marcus wasn't so sure that Cliff would be and he hadn't been feeling how Cliff treated him lately. Once they started fucking around, Cliff treated him like a bitch and that shit was going to come to an end.

"Marcus, did you hear me?" Red shouted.

Marcus hit the blunt and replied, "My bad, sis, I was over here tripping. Text Cliff and tell him to slide through."

"I'm a step ahead of you. If we gone do this, it's going to have to be tomorrow night before they return," Red confirmed.

Leaving Marcus in the living room, Red went into her room, undressed from the club attire and slipped in something more comfortable.

Power of the Pie

Chapter 19

For the last week the team had been trying to finish off unfinished business. Jack put a bounty on Marcus' head. Between him and Lamont, they had recruited one hundred more hungry soldiers to join the squad. Of course Cliff wasn't feeling it because he was knocked down even more after complaining about his position within the company. Cliff wasn't tripping, though. After meeting with Red and Marcus, he was in on the idea of robbing POP's main house. He had no clue to where it was, but Red knew the ins and outs.

While the girls were out of town meeting with the connect, Jack had tightened up on everything and was hoping that before his right hand man went out of town, shit would be taken care of. Leaving the house, tired of hearing Alicia's mouth about where he had been and with who, he picked up Lamont and headed to the strip club. Right now he needed to clear his head and he realized that nothing was better than seeing some hoes shake their ass and drink.

"My nigga, you looking bad. You straight?" Lamont asked.

Jack looked out the window and replied, "I'm good. Alicia's ass is stressing me the fuck out with all the twenty one questions. It's like she forgot what we do and what's at stake."

"Alicia is a ruthless one. She hasn't forgotten and regardless of how good she is in these streets, she is still a female. A female with emotions. Worry when you got a bitch that don't care and her only concern is how much dough you getting," Lamont explained.

Pulling into the parking lot of the strip club, Jack sparked up a blunt and sent a text to Alicia apologizing.

Jack: Boo, I'm sorry I stormed out like that. You know what it is and what a nigga have to do. Make sure when I get home you're naked. ☐ lol"

Security was tight inside, there was a special performer who went by the name of Thunder thighs. After shooting the security guard some dough to get in with their pieces, Lamont went to the bar and paid for the biggest VIP. The one that was was front center of the stage and nothing but the top ranking strippers were allowed in VIP.

Before even sitting down, nothing but the best bottles were on the table. For Lamont, it was Hennessey and Jack was sipping on the Patron. Ten minutes passed before the main act came on stage. Jack and Lamont were drooling and wanted private dances.

Thunder walked out on stage wearing an all-black, lace cat suit with black eight inch stilettoes and her hair high in a bun. Glancing around the room as she crawled on the floor to get a good look at the audience, Thunder noticed Jack and Lamont. That meant money was in the building.

She'd been trying to get with Lamont before she hooked up with Isaac but with no such luck. From what she heard in the streets, Lamont came home from jail getting his bread up and was single. Staring him down until she had his eyes on hers, Thunder pretended it was just those two in the room and danced her ass off. By the end of the song she was ass naked and playing with the kitty.

All the men were whistling and hollering. Thinking of Lamont fucking her right there made her bust a nut. If it wasn't for the DJ interrupting, the show would've continued.

Getting up, Thunder looked around a little embarrassed. Picking up the money from the floor, she made her way back to the dressing room. As she was sitting at her station, the bartender came to the back and said a private dance was requested. Hopping in the shower to take a fast hoe bath, Thunder quickly cleaned herself up, changed, and walked to the VIP.

"You requested a private dance?" Thunder asked Lamont, walking into the VIP.

Lamont hit the drink and responded, "Hell yeah. This is my boy Jack, I'm Lamont. And you are?"

"Thunder is the stage name, but my real name is Jasmine." Thunder gestured.

Thunder a.k.a Jasmine sat on his lap and began giving him a private dance and Jack excused himself. Jasmine was doing everything possible to make Lamont hard and her planned worked. By the end of the song, Lamont was begging to take her to the motel. Jasmine played like she wasn't interested before finally giving in.

"Jasmine, go change and meet me out front," Lamont recommended.

"Snow gon' kick your ass," Jack joked, exiting the club.

Lamont thought about it. They weren't official yet. "Me and Snow haven't made shit official. You gon' be straight?"

"I'm good, going home to the wifey and get me some. Be straight, you can't trust these hoes. I would hate to wake up tomorrow to you on the news," Jack advised.

Jack got into his car and waited until he knew his boy was straight. Seeing that he was cool, he made his way home. Jack and Snow's house was in the cuts, in the back by the Sleep Train Arena. He loved living in the neighborhood because it was highly patrolled by security. Nothing but lawyers and doctors lived in the area.

Once inside the house, Jack realized how drunk he was when he fell. He'd forgotten about the step when you first enter the house. Just as he was getting up and laughing, Alicia turned the hall light on and asked, "You gon' just stand there laughing at yourself? Or are you gon' come get this pussy?"

Taking off his shoes, Jack couldn't believe what stood before his eyes. His queen was standing there naked, glistening in baby oil with seven inch red bottoms on. Alicia's hair was pulled up in a messy pony tail and she wore a little bit of makeup and the diamond earrings he gave her.

During the process of walking towards Alicia, Jack started removing his clothes. No words were said as he picked her up and carried her up the stairs to their bedroom. Inside, there were rose petals that traced the room, candles lit and soft melodies playing in the background.

Lying her down, Jack started kissing and worshiping the body of his goddess. Opening her legs so he could get a full view of her pearl, he dove in like I man looking for gold. As he tasted her sweet nectar, Jack was surprised when he tasted the honey that dripped from her insides.

Tonight Alicia had decided that there would be no more bitching at her man, only love and friendship. She wanted to develop a partnership and Jack was the perfect man for the job.

On the other side of town, Lamont was at Motel 6 off of Richards with Jasmine. The two were up until the crack of dawn fucking like teenagers.

Finally Irvin had made it to the meeting. Snow was beyond annoyed at the audacity of him to show up an hour late. Each woman had been on their game. Javier was trying to fill them up with alcohol to get them drunk. The ladies refused every attempt and sipped on water instead. When they first came into the game they were a little naïve, but in time they knew it like the back of their hands and they trusted no one.

"Ladies, I am so sorry to keep you. Please forgive me," Irvin said before sitting down.

Alexis smirked, "Why, of course, Irvin."

"Father, I was just telling the ladies about how we're loving their numbers within the last few weeks," Javier spoke to his father.

"That we are, ladies. The reason I called you down her is because I have heard that you have a bit of trouble," Irvin argued.

Jordan took a sip of water. "Irvin, you knew like we did, some were going to test us being new to the game and all."

"But the little trouble we have will be wrapped up soon enough," Snow added.

"So now you're running four separate territories. Don't you ladies think that's a bit much?" Irvin questioned.

Snow looked at Irvin and then at Javier. "Like my sister was saying, this problem is small and we can assure you it's handled. Yes, we are running four locations and we have it all under control. Our teams have tripled with workers and soldiers."

"Okay, as long as nothing comes my way and the money continues to flow, were good," Irvin confirmed.

"Glad to hear it. Now can we enjoy some of this good food and continue making these coins?" Jordan held up her glass, proposing a toast.

For a second Irvin hesitated, then replied, "Let's eat."

Through the remainder of the meal, the group talked about good investments and new politicians. Afterwards, the ladies said their goodbyes and headed back to the hotel. Instead of going straight to the hotel, though, Jordan pulled into the gas station and scanned the car.

She wanted to make sure nothing like a tracking device or a recorder had been added to the vehicle.

Coming up from the ground smiling, she felt like it was official. The connection really was going to allow them to handle things and continue doing business. Rather than allowing the valet to park the truck, Jordan parked in the rear and made her way inside. Once inside of the room, Snow went to the phone and called up room service. Alexis went to the bar and poured the ladies some drinks. She was ecstatic that the meeting went well.

"I'm too happy that we found a better house then the last one," Jordan said.

Alexis took off her shoes and replied, "Yeah, me too. And it's in the cuts with the best security money can buy."

"Is everything out of the old spot?" Snow asked.

"Well, no. All the big shit, yeah," Jordan answered.

Before Alexis could speak there was a knock at the door, it was the attendant with their meal. Sitting at the table, they bowed their heads and said a prayer.

Alexis blurted out, "I'm too happy, Shit went well in the meeting."

"Same here," Snow agreed.

"Sis, what's wrong with you? Why you not eating?" Alexis questioned.

"You two know me, I can't kick back until this unfinished business comes to an end. Plus, I miss my man," Jordan disclosed.

Getting up from the table, Snow went into the closet and started packing up her clothes.

"What you doing?" Alexis barked.

"Sis, is right. We will celebrate when we put an end to these double crossing as muthafuckas," Snow said before going into the bathroom to change into something more comfortable for the road.

An hour later the ladies checked out of the Marriot and were on the highway headed home. A few hours away from Sacramento, Alexis awakened the girls. On her way to the new house, Jordan realized that she need to get her boxes from their old home.

For the past few hours Red had been awake, putting the plan together. Cliff told her that Jordan and the other girls weren't due back home for the next few days. Staking out their house she saw that there wasn't the normal traffic going in and out.

Their plan was solid proof, Red still remembered the code to the safe and hoped like hell it was still the same. Parked a block away from the house in Jasmine's car, the four waited for the perfect time to break in. Cliff had come through with a few straps and ski masks. When coming up with the idea to rob POP, Red had no idea what all was needed. Even though the crew turned their backs on her and put her out, she didn't want to see anyone get hurt.

Leaving shit in Jasmine and Marcus' hands was out of the question. They were out for blood, each seeking revenge for feeling betrayed when in Red's mind they both had gotten what they deserved.

Cliff opened the back door to the car and whispered, "Y'all ready?"

"Hell yeah, let's do this!" Jasmine's adrenaline was pumping.

Marcus was in a zone, talking to himself. "Everybody can get it, if there smart they will just hand over the money."

All four tiptoed up the street and into the yard of the house in which they were getting ready to rob.

Exiting East Commerce, headed towards POP old headquarters, Alexis blasted Lil Boosie's Life after Deathrow and was feeling the words Boosie was spitting. Turning down there street, something in Jordan's gut told her something wasn't right. She cut the lights off and drove down the street slowly.

Snow blurted out, "Who the fuck is that on the side of the house?"

"I don't know, but they look like there up to no good," Jordan mumbled.

Alexis yelled, "Oh, shit! There is one on the other side too."

Jordan demanded, "Park this shit around the corner and get them thangs ready."

Turning down Di Vinci Way, Alexis parked the car and laced up her tennis shoes. Checking their weapons, each was strapped and ready for whatever.

"We can hop over Mr. Johnson's gate," Snow whispered.

Going over the gate one by one, they finally reached their yard and were sure to be as silent as possible, not wanting to alert whoever was there. Seeing the back door window had been broken, Jordan put her hands to her lips and went inside with Snow and Alexis on her heels.

The voices could be heard coming from the basement. Whoever was there knew where the safe was hidden. Alexis could hear a female voice that sounded all too familiar. Snow recognized it as well.

Jordan whispered, "Is that who the fuck I think it is?"

Snow shook her head up and down, confirming Jordan's suspicion. There was more than one pair of footsteps being heard upstairs and voices coming from the basement. Taking the steps from the kitchen one at a time, the three were ready to start shooting.

Jordan kicked the door in and they all started busting, not giving a fuck who it was.

BOOM! BOOM! BOOM!

One was hit in the shoulders and their body flew backfrom the impact of the .45. Jasmine ran as fast as her legs would allow her through the bathroom and down the stairs. Snow and Alexis rushed behind her and the other intruders, letting there canons spit with no such luck at getting the others.

Making their way back up the stairs with Jordan, they saw that she was standing over the body and was shocked by what she saw when she removed the mask.

"Muthafucka too hard to think you could come in my shit and rob me." Tears were cascading down Jordan's face.

Snow walked over to her sister and looked at the trespasser. Without second thought she said before pulling the trigger, "You picked the wrong fucking people to rob."

POW! POW!

Made in the USA
Middletown, DE
12 August 2022

70617302R00126